"What happened?" he persisted

His eyes flashed over her from head to toe in appreciation.

Before Becky could do more than open her mouth, the flight attendant interrupted them, beaming. "Oh, so you do know one another! Small world isn't it?"

"A small world." Stirling hadn't taken his eyes off Rebecca. "You don't think I could have forgotten your face, do you? You might have changed physically, and drastically at that, but those emerald eyes of yours, they could never change."

The pretence was over. Becky moved her shoulder away, resenting his touch. "Do me a favor, Stirling, spare me the charm. It doesn't suit you. You might have been exceedingly cruel ten years ago, but at least you were honest then."

Claudia Jameson lives in Berkshire, England, with her husband and family. She is an extremely popular author in both the Harlequin Presents and Harlequin Romance series. And no wonder! Her lively dialogue and ingenious plots—with the occasional dash of suspense—make her a favorite with romance readers everywhere.

Books by Claudia Jameson

HARLEQUIN ROMANCE

HARLEQUIN PRESENTS

Don't miss any of our special offers. Write to us at the following address for information on our newest releases.

Harlequin Reader Service
P.O. Box 1397, Buffalo, NY 14240
Canadian address: P.O. Box 603,
Fort Erie, Ont. L2A 5X3

A LOVE
THAT ENDURES

Claudia Jameson

Harlequin Books

TORONTO • NEW YORK • LONDON
AMSTERDAM • PARIS • SYDNEY • HAMBURG
STOCKHOLM • ATHENS • TOKYO • MILAN
MADRID • WARSAW • BUDAPEST • AUCKLAND

For Stefan, for Otto and for Switzerland

Original hardcover edition published in 1991
by Mills & Boon Limited

ISBN 0-373-03189-0

Harlequin Romance first edition April 1992

A LOVE THAT ENDURES

CHAPTER ONE

'WHAT a gorgeous suntan!'

Rebecca Hill opened her eyes to see a smiling stewardess holding out a tray on which there were several glasses of champagne. Champagne, and the plane's doors had not yet been closed for take-off; it was still standing on the tarmac of New York's J.F. Kennedy airport.

It was great to fly first-class—not that she would have spent that sort of money on herself, in spite of the fat fees she'd been earning for some time. She had better things to do with her money; with an eye to the future she was saving far more than she was spending. Besides, flying first-class was *very* expensive.

The company had paid for the tickets to and from America—for hers, for Ingrid's and for the rest of the team's. She smiled as she thought of the riotous journey they'd all had together several weeks ago. They had all flown from London to Los Angeles direct but this flight back to London was going to be different. Becky, as her friends called her, was alone now.

'Thank you.' She accepted the compliment and the champagne gracefully, glancing around, wondering why they were not yet airborne. 'What's the delay? We should be on our way by now.' The first-class section was half-empty, everyone had boarded over half an hour ago, but there was still no sign of the plane taking off. 'Is there engine trouble or something?'

As if in answer a voice came over the PA system. It was only when she heard it that Becky realised she'd heard the same announcement a little earlier. But she had been half-asleep then; she had fallen into a doze the moment she'd relaxed in the plush, comfortable window-seat. She listened now, wondering what had happened to the Mr Robard who appeared to have gone missing. He was being asked to report to the chief steward.

'It happens.' The stewardess was smiling again, shrugging as if she hadn't a care in the world. 'We're a passenger short. His luggage was checked in, he's on our list, but he hasn't materialised yet.'

'Well, it's very inconsiderate of him, whoever he is. I have a connection to make when I get to London. Mind you, I have got two hours to spare.'

'Don't worry, we won't be delayed that long. So what about your suntan? Did you get it in New York?'

'No. Hardly! The weather here has been awful this past week, though I'm told it's usually quite decent at this time of year.'

It was the beginning of October and it was raining again now, streaming steadily down the window by which Becky was sitting. She glanced back at the stewardess, glad to see that as yet there was no one in the seat next to her, hoping that it had not been allocated to the missing passenger. With a little luck it would stay empty, and she would be able to put the armrest up, put her feet up and sleep away the next few hours. It was a blissful thought. She had been working hard and she'd been playing hard. The past week in New York had been hectic, to say the least.

'Awful?' The stewardess was British, friendly and obviously content to chat about the weather. 'I wouldn't know, I've been on a different run these past few weeks.'

'Well, I've been in California—hence the suntan. It was lovely there, day after day of glorious sunshine.'

'And you were on holiday, basking in it!'

'Oh, no.' Becky shook her head very firmly. 'I was working like an idiot in California, believe me. This past week—well, almost a week—I've been in New York on what was supposed to be the start of a holiday.'

'But it was exhausting, right?' There was a knowing smile. 'I know, New York is like that, especially when it's your first experience and you're trying to see all the sights.'

'It was—and I did!' Rebecca laughed, remembering. Her days with Michael McCaffrey had been exhausting, and fun. And wet. She thought of him with fondness, wondering whether it was the Irish blood in him that made him so charming... and crazy. He certainly liked to live it up, not that she was complaining. She had had a super time with him, and with his friends. When he had proposed marriage, just three days after she'd been introduced to him, she had laughed so hard she'd given herself a stitch. And when he'd insisted that he was serious she had laughed all the harder.

Her laughter faded. To think there had been a time when she'd been so unpopular, when she had been an ugly duckling. An ugly duckling? She had been downright fat. And spotty. And inhibited and unsure about her future. No one had understood that, though, or so it had seemed at the time. Oh, her parents had loved her, as had her older brother and sister, but they hadn't understood what had been going on inside her, they hadn't protected her from all the teasing she'd had as a teenager.

It hadn't felt like teasing, either, it had felt like victimisation, and some memories hadn't faded in spite of the years that had passed since then. Some memories—like those of her brother's friend, for example. He had picked

on her and he should have known better because he had
been so much older. Of course she could look back now,
from the standpoint of maturity, and see how the man's
taunting had in fact helped her—but that didn't elim-
inate the very real distress she had felt as a youngster.

She shook herself, wondering why she was even
bothering to think about that man, wondering why he
was suddenly in her mind after all these years.

Hers was a different story now, a very different story.
Life was nothing less than ideal, for the time being at
least, and she was a success. Exhausted or not, Rebecca
was on top of the world. The past four years as a model
had been an education; she had learnt more in the past
four years than she ever had in school, about life, about
people. She was twenty-three years old and was currently in great demand, working with the biggest London
agency and getting plum jobs which often took her
overseas. But she had never been to New York before,
which was why she had stopped over to spend a few days
there.

'Madam?' The stewardess was back with a tray of hors
d'oeuvres and a menu that looked interesting. 'And can
I get you another glass of champagne?'

'No, thanks. What I'd really like is to see this big bird
flying.'

There was a sympathetic nod. 'Please don't worry
about your connection, you'll make it. Are you off on
another assignment?'

'Assignment?' Becky laughed. 'How did you know?'

'That you're a model?' The eyes of the stewardess were
twinkling, amused. 'Oh, one gets to know these things
in this job. Anyhow, it wasn't exactly difficult to spot.
If you don't mind my saying so, your casual clothes are

no disguise for your figure. As for your face and your hair—I suppose you do photographic work?'

Becky shrugged. Her looks had never gone to her head, nor would they ever. The ugly duckling might have grown into a beautiful swan but she did not take it for granted. 'I do whatever the clients want me to do. Within reason,' she added, seeing the brows of the older woman go up in mock amusement. 'We've just been shooting on location for a manufacturer of hair products—no expense spared. It's a whole new campaign and they used a dozen girls ranging from blondes through to brunettes—all shades.'

Rebecca was a brunette. Her hair was almost, but not quite, black. Her friend Ingrid was as blonde as they come and, like Becky's, her hair had never seen a bottle of dye or a rinse.

'I knew you had to be doing something glamorous for a living.'

'What? You have to be joking!' These so-called glamour jobs were hard work, and this woman should have known better. 'That's what people say about airline stewardesses, isn't it? That their work is glamorous?'

There was open laughter now. 'Sorry, I couldn't resist the tease.' She looked heavenwards, as if remembering with a mixture of pleasure and pain. 'I do know how it is—I used to be a model. I didn't do much photographic work, though; I mainly modelled clothes and that was hard enough. So what's your next assignment?'

'There isn't one.' Becky's smile was almost smug. 'At least, not until I'm ready. I'm going on to Switzerland, to stay with a friend and her family. It's going to be a real, honest-to-goodness holiday.'

'You mean the sort where you can sleep during the day, if that's what you want to do?'

'Exactly! My girlfriend had promised not to hassle me, to let me sleep all day every day.'

'But you won't,' the stewardess said seriously. 'Not unless you've seen all there is to see in Switzerland.'

'I haven't. I haven't been there before.'

'Not at all? Not even for the skiing?'

'I have been skiing but never, as it happens, in Switzerland.'

'Well, there's no snow now, of course, but there's so much to see, it's very beautiful in the autumn and it—excuse me.' She was interrupted, or rather she interrupted herself, by the sudden appearance of a tall, broad, blond-haired man. Becky had only the barest glance at him before he was obscured from her view by the stewardess; she could see only that he was wearing an immaculately cut business suit and that he looked very much like a first-class fare. An executive of some sort. He was the missing passenger, no doubt.

He sat in the window-seat adjacent to Becky but across the aisle, immediately opening a newspaper and sticking it in front of his face. He was, presumably, embarrassed by the delay he'd caused. Rebecca hoped so. There was no opportunity for her to glare at him and let her displeasure be known. That one passenger could hold up a flight for so long seemed a bit rich to her. The stewardess was still talking to him, offering him a glass of champagne which he refused. All Rebecca could see across the aisle was half of his profile—but there was something vaguely familiar about it. Wasn't there? Had she seen him somewhere in New York, perhaps? In a restaurant or something?

She thought no more about it. Within half an hour she was sound asleep and the plane was speeding on its way to London.

Some time later she was wakened by the same stewardess, with an apology this time. 'I'm sorry to disturb you but you did say you'd like a meal. Unless I'm told specifically not to wake someone——'

What the rest of the sentence was, Becky had no idea. Her eyes were wide open and staring—staring at the man across the aisle. She could not believe what she was seeing. She recognised him at once, but *instantly*! No wonder she'd thought there was something familiar about that bit of profile!

Robard. Why hadn't she recognised the name?

The stewardess was saying something about headphones and the in-flight movie but Becky didn't hear that, either. Robard. Stirling *Robard*. She had recognised it at some level of her mind, she must have, because two minutes after hearing the name she had been thinking about him, about her childhood, about the pain he had caused her.

And here he was—sitting across the aisle from her!

'What? Sorry, I didn't hear you.' She was speaking to the stewardess but her eyes were still on the man. He was asleep and she was very glad of that. But for how long had he been asleep? Had he recognised her? Had he been looking at her while she had been sleeping? The idea of that was unwelcome but, happily, she was no longer vulnerable, no longer labouring under the agonies of a teenage crush. She was ten years older than she had been when she first met him and she was an extremely different person with an extremely different character.

With a look of amusement the stewardess followed Becky's eyes, letting her own eyes feast for a moment before she turned back. She bent low, ensuring no one else could hear. 'He is gorgeous, isn't he?'

Becky laughed as if she had said something highly amusing. Of their own volition her eyes moved back to the sleeping figure. Gorgeous? She couldn't see it. Oh, she had once thought so, and then some, when first she had set eyes on him, but she couldn't see it now and she said as much. 'I don't see it myself, so this must be a case of one man's meat or something. He—I thought I knew him, actually,' she added. 'The name was Robard, wasn't it?'

'That's right. Stirling Robard.'

Becky looked down at her hands. Why had she asked, why had she said that? She knew very well what his name was, there was no mistake. She would never forget that face, and in any case he had hardly changed, unlike her. He had to be—what?—in his middle thirties now. He was older than Ian, her brother. Stirling had started university late and had become a friend of Ian's there. And Ian, bless him, had looked up to him with such regard! He had brought Stirling home to stay during the holidays—and she recalled only too well every one of those occasions.

Ian hadn't mentioned the man's name for years. The two of them had lost touch long since, Becky had no idea why; just one of those things, probably. They had gone their separate ways after leaving university and that was that.

'I daren't wake him,' the stewardess was saying. 'He told me he didn't want anything to eat or drink, he said that all he wanted was some sleep.'

Becky laughed again at the apology in her voice. 'That's quite all right, it's not an acquaintance I'm eager to renew. In fact I might be mistaken,' she added, lying deliberately to put an end to the conversation. 'I thought I knew the name but I can't say I know the face.'

Throughout her meal, however, she kept glancing across the aisle at that face, feeling undeniably agitated to the point where she had to remind herself that she could now easily handle the Stirling Robards of this world—and that there was no chance of his recognising her anyway.

When the in-flight movie came on, she put on her headphones and relaxed . . . and then the man across the aisle stirred in his sleep, his long legs rearranging themselves.

At that point Rebecca put her seatbelt aside and went upstairs to the lounge, gratified to discover that there were several empty seats up there, too. She ordered a drink from the steward and sat nursing it, acknowledging that she was not quite as self-contained as she should be. She had not wanted to run the risk of Stirling recognising her, she had not wanted to get into conversation with him. But why? Maybe she hadn't put the past into perspective, after all . . .

By the age of twelve she had been grossly overweight and her life at senior school had been a misery. She had been useless at games, she had been ostracised because of her appearance and she had been picked on for dragging behind academically. In other words she hadn't been able to get anything right. It had been too awful for words, all her failings—while her older brother and sister, Ian and Susan, had been brilliant and handsome, brilliant and beautiful respectively. It had been sickening, the way her parents had so often held them up as examples, unaware that this made her feel worse.

Although she had been the afterthought in the family, born several years later than her brother and sister, in honesty she could not say she had ever felt unloved, not by her parents and not by her siblings. She had, however, felt angry at their lack of understanding. To be fair, Ian and Susan had both attempted to reassure her, but telling her she was sweet and pretty had been no consolation, no compensation for the failure she felt, for the friends she lacked.

And then Stirling Robard had entered her life. Rebecca had fallen crazily head-over-heels in love with her brother's friend the moment she'd set eyes on him, thinking him the most beautiful man she had ever seen. That was why his taunts had hurt so, of course; because she had cared so very much what he thought of her. He was there during most of the university holidays, a stranger, one who lived in and treated her home as if it were his own.

'Instead of complaining,' he'd said once, 'why don't you do something about yourself?' It had been during dinner and all the family had been present—but that hadn't deterred him.

Nothing had deterred him. 'Rebecca, if you really *don't* want to look like a little dumpling, why do you gorge yourself so much? Are you aware that that's your sixth potato—or have you stopped counting?'

And what had her father said? 'She's always had a good appetite, Stirling. I like to see youngsters eating well—but I suppose you could be right.'

Cut to the quick by the young man's cruelty, by her father's failure to protect her from his taunts, Rebecca had been unable to speak. Instead she had fumed, her love for Stirling Robard turning instantly to hatred...only to change back again in time...and back yet again.

She had felt both murderous and impotent on many occasions. One such was the time he ordered her to wash her hair. She remembered it very clearly; it had happened one Sunday morning, no one else had been in earshot and she had retaliated for once, but it had been to no avail.

'Leave me alone, you! You're always picking on me!' She had been emerging from the bathroom and Stirling had cornered her. 'I will *not* go back in there. I will *not* wash my hair.'

'OK,' he shrugged, 'then leave it lank and greasy, looking as if it belongs on the end of a mop.'

'Yes, I will. Now shift yourself, get out of my way.'

'Fine. Rebel if you must. You'll be anything but yourself, won't you? And you'll do nothing to help yourself, do nothing to improve your appearance. You'll just keep on moaning about it.'

She burst into tears from sheer frustration. 'Get away from me! There's nothing I *can* do, don't you see? I'm fat and plain and I'm stuck with it!'

'Rubbish! You know, your sister is——'

'*Don't!* I don't want to hear it!' Rebecca's anger overwhelmed her. Without knowing what she was doing, she kicked him swiftly on the shin. Unfortunately she had forgotten she was barefoot and it hurt her more than it had hurt him. Stirling didn't move a muscle; he just leaned against the landing wall and watched as she grabbed her painful toes, almost hissing at him in her fury. 'I don't want to hear about how beautiful Susan is, I don't want to hear how clever she is! And I don't want to talk to you ever again!'

'When you've quite finished,' he said, looking down at her as if she were mad, 'I shall go on. I was about to say that your sister is an extremely attractive girl, but she's not half as nice-looking as you. Do you know that?'

'Get stuffed!'

'Which brings me to my point nicely. If you'd just have a little respect for yourself, if you'd just cut down on the monstrous meals you stuff down, not to mention the unending supply of sweets and cakes you get through, you could be a little beauty. It's all there, the potential; all it needs is a chance to make itself seen.'

In reply she swore at him, using words she would never have used in front of her parents.

'Oh,' he mocked, 'I'm highly impressed by that, Rebecca. Words of one syllable, yet. How clever you are!'

Silence.

'You know, I'm very tempted to put you over my knee. But I suspect that would be counter-productive. I think the best way of getting through to you is to tell you you're not fooling *me* for one minute. You act dumb, you get lousy reports from school, but you and I know different, don't we? You see, I've noticed a few things about you—I happen to know that you really are clever. For example, I saw you complete the crossword in *The Times* the other day when your father left it unfinished. So what game is it you're playing? Why are you constantly seeking attention through negativity when you could just as easily——'

'Attention? I don't want attention! That's just my point, you idiot. All I want is to be left alone. I want *you* to stop picking on me, I want——'

'You don't know what you want. That's your trouble. You're just wallowing in your negativity. It's an appalling waste.'

'And it's none of your business!' Rebecca tried to get away from him then, she straightened and made to walk past him, but he caught hold of her and pinned her to the wall.

'Back into the bathroom,' he said. 'Go on. We're all going out to lunch today and you look a mess.'

At thirteen she had not known how to fight him any further. She had given in because she had felt him immovable, even more stubborn than she had been.

It had been like that every time she saw him; he picked and prodded, he nagged and goaded her until the day came when her anger with him finally turned inwards. She reached a point when she became as angry with herself as she was with him. She didn't know it at the time but it was in fact the last day she would see him. It just after Easter during the year he and Ian graduated from university.

Had she known he was not coming back during the summer, she might not have undertaken her campaign. As it was she almost starved herself during the weeks that followed. Her parents, at a loss to understand the change in her behaviour, became almost frantic and talked in alarm of anorexia. Rebecca was in no danger of that, though; there was no way she would allow herself to become ill. What she wanted was to shed her excess weight and no more; what she wanted was to be like other girls of her age.

But what she wanted most of all was for Stirling to admire her instead of criticising her.

So she slimmed. And slimmed. And within a few months her entire life changed because of it. Her confidence grew, she began to be herself, she made friends and let herself behave in class as she never had before, answering questions, gaining good marks and doing well in exams. At the same time, she shot up in height. And still she slimmed. By the time she left school she was five feet eight and the ideal weight for her height. Alas, she never had the satisfaction of Stirling seeing her after her transformation.

Until today.

Now, she looked out at the sky and smiled inwardly, unable to deny that he had been the catalyst that changed her life. She should feel grateful to him—but she didn't.

At length she fell asleep again, waking to the sound of the captain's voice announcing their arrival at Heathrow in approximately twenty-two minutes. Good. There was time to brush her teeth and tidy up. She went downstairs to get the travel bag she had stowed—only to find herself face to face with Stirling.

'Excuse me.' She looked away from him, proud of the casualness in her voice as she stepped aside to let him pass. She did not look back at him; instead she reached in the overhead locker to retrieve her bag.

'Allow me, Rebecca.' There was a hand on her shoulder, a hand reaching for her bag, and suddenly she was breathing a little too heavily. Why, she had no idea. He couldn't affect her now—her confidence was not easily shaken these days, not by any means. Perhaps she was just irked that he had recognised her when she was so very, very different from the girl he had last seen.

She composed herself at once. 'I'm sorry,' she said, her smile ready but distant. 'Have we met?'

He didn't even answer that. He let his slate-grey eyes lock on to hers and he smiled, that slow smile she remembered only too well. How she had loved it once...and hated it! 'Surely you can do better than that, Rebecca? I haven't changed much. I'm a little older and a little wiser, of course, but that's about it.'

'I'm sorry,' she said again, making to move away. 'You must be mistaken. I'm afraid I don't know you.'

The last thing Becky expected was merriment. She felt sure she would have created doubt in his mind. She was wrong. He threw back his head and roared with laughter. 'Good lord! Did you resent me that badly? And do you still? What happened?' he persisted, his eyes flicking over her from top to toe. 'Did you forget to grow up during the past ten years?'

Opening her mouth to answer was as far as she got. The stewardess interrupted them, beaming. 'Ah, so you do know one another!' She turned to Stirling, nodding in Becky's direction. 'Miss Hill thought she knew you. I mean she knew your name but she wasn't sure about your face. It's a small world, isn't it?' she added before moving away.

'A small world.' Stirling hadn't taken his eyes off Rebecca. 'As for faces, you don't think I could have forgotten yours, do you? You might have changed physically, and drastically at that, but those emerald eyes of yours, they could never change. Your eyes, and those lovely high cheekbones...'

The pretence was over. Becky moved her shoulder away, resenting his touch. 'Do me a favour, Stirling: spare me the charm, it doesn't suit you. You might have been a bastard ten years ago but at least you were *honest* then.'

'A bastard?'

'A bastard.' She repeated the word without apology, without hesitation. 'An insensitive one at that.'

He was laughing again. 'Oh, come on! Someone had to point out the error of your ways. Much as I liked them, your parents never did—they spoiled you rotten. How are they, by the way? And Ian and Susan?'

With that he put his hand on her again, on her arm this time. It was a gesture of friendliness she didn't welcome; the warmth of his lean fingers felt like an invasion through the fine wool of her sweater. 'Everyone's well,' she snapped. 'Now let me go, please. I'm trying to get to the loo before we land.'

'They're all occupied,' he informed her. 'But there's plenty of time, not to worry. You're still uptight, I see. Still lacking a sense of humour, too.'

'I was never uptight, I was never lacking a sense of humour. I was an unhappy, pubescent teenager—and you never had the sensitivity to realise it.'

'Didn't I? Have you ever stopped to think——?'

'Oh, I know it was all a long time ago, and I seem to recall that you had your own problems then, but that does not exonerate you in my eyes.'

'In your eyes?' He didn't let her go—his hand was still on her arm, firmer in its hold now. He was neither amused nor annoyed, he was merely looking steadily at her. 'I suggest you open those eyes, Rebecca Hill. When you look in the mirror, assuming you see what I see, you should ask yourself a question or two. Look at you; you're tall and slim and beautiful now. What harm did I ever do you? What was wrong in my pointing out that you could help yourself?'

'Nothing.' It came grudgingly and she turned and walked away, heading with dignity in the direction of the lavatory.

When she returned to her seat for their landing, she kept her eyes front. Maybe she was being childish but she couldn't seem to stop herself.

Like everyone else, Stirling had to wait for his luggage once they got inside the airport terminal. Like everyone else he had to go through Customs—and he was at Becky's side when he did so. 'Look, Rebecca—why don't you come and have a cup of coffee with me? I've got a meeting in the City this afternoon but I can spare an hour or so.'

She almost laughed. Was she supposed to be flattered by that? It was just about noon, English time, and for one thing she was still feeling exhausted. This, before jet-lag had set in. 'No, thank you, I have no time to— spare, as you so charmingly put it. I'm catching a plane to Zurich, I have several telephone calls to make, and I have to get to another terminal.'

'Zurich?'

'It's in Switzerland.' She glanced at him, pleased by his obvious annoyance.

He nodded, slowly, as if he had her measure. 'So you haven't changed much inwardly. You're still something of a brat and I still have a strong inclination to put you over my knee and paddle your behind.'

That remark wasn't even worthy of a retort. Becky just carried on regardless. 'Yes, Switzerland. You know, that place between Italy and France and Germany and Austria. Are you with it now? I'm going to Lucerne, actually, to a party.' She added this with a deliberate toss of her head, letting her long mane of darkest brown hair go flying silkily about her. It always looked good like that on photographs, it always drew attention.

It drew his. He was looking at her now as if he'd never seen her before. 'You're going to Lucerne for a party?'

'Why so surprised, Stirling? I live life to the fullest these days. The ugly duckling, or in your own words the "little dumpling", is no more.'

'And what has she turned into?' he asked, his eyes narrowing in a way that made her uneasy for some reason. Suddenly she wanted to explain further, to erase the wrong impression she had deliberately given him.

'It's an anniversary party, the parents of a friend of mine.' Her voice was without sarcasm but she got no response at all. 'I mean a girlfriend, another model.'

That got a response; it was a look of open disapproval. 'Another model? Is that what you do?'

'For what it's worth, I happen to be a very successful model.' She was being defensive. Why? Because he was still looking sceptical and she still felt the need to explain herself? Perhaps it was because she was also regretting her childishness with him earlier. 'It provides me with a very good living. I—my friend Ingrid Bachmann and I are both with the same agency in London and we've spent the past few weeks in the States doing ads. Ingrid is Swiss and she hasn't been home for almost two years. She left California last week to go home and be with her parents alone for a bit. I spent a few days in New York and I said I'd get to Lucerne in time for the party on Saturday. Stirling? What's so amusing?'

She could make no sense of the man. He was laughing his head off, telling her nothing. He was laughing so hard that she almost laughed with him. Almost. But she caught sight of a clock on the wall and she discovered that her time, and her patience, was running out. 'Good grief, look at the time! If you've quite finished having hysterics, I'll say goodbye. *Goodbye.*'

And with that, for the second time, she walked away from him, pushing her luggage trolley in front of her and keeping her eyes front. Nevertheless she heard his final words to her, low and softly spoken though they were.

'No, *au revoir*, Rebecca. Oh, I much prefer *au revoir*!'

CHAPTER TWO

'SUSAN? Hi, it's me. What? Sorry about the noise, I'm in a call-box at Heathrow. I just tried to ring Mum and Dad but there was no answer. Gone shopping, probably.' Becky smiled at the thought. Her father had never been domesticated but since his early retirement he helped his wife with her chores as much as he could. 'I called Ian at his office but he was out, too. Gone to lunch.'

'So I'm your last resort, eh?'

'Susan——'

'That was a joke.'

'Oh.' Becky sighed inwardly. Admittedly her sense of humour seemed to have deserted her today. 'Sorry, I'm not in the best of moods. For one thing I'm tired.'

'And for another?' her sister asked. 'What's up? You don't sound right. Are you ill?'

'No, no.' For another thing she was having a slight twinge of conscience. Her days between California and Switzerland could have been spent at home in Colchester; her family had wanted that but—well, a visit to New York had been irresistible. She wouldn't have missed it but, there again, it would have been nice to go home and have a few days of normality. She was certainly looking forward to the rest and the tranquillity in store in Lucerne.

'Rebecca? Are you still there?' There was a hint of alarm in Susan's voice.

'I'm here, and I'm absolutely fine, I promise you. It's just the travelling——'

'The *travelling*! I hope that isn't a complaint? I'd give my eye-teeth to have half of all you have. Hold on a minute, it sounds as if Sally's doing something terrible to the cat...'

Rebecca held on, knowing what her sister was going to say next—it was a routine they had been through before. Susan envied Becky's lifestyle, or said she did, and just occasionally Becky envied Susan's. There were moments when she wanted the stability of a home, a home of her own. A home in the country, perhaps, somewhere or something other than the rented house she shared in London with Ingrid and two other models; a house which was invaded nightly by phone calls and boyfriends and sundry droppers-in. All in all, though, her life was great—but it couldn't go on at this pace forever, she was aware of that much. If nothing else, her looks wouldn't last forever. Twenty-three was pretty old for the sort of work she did, and it was for these reasons that she was saving every bit of her spare money—eventually to invest in a business.

She fed more money into the telephone box and imagined the goings-on in her sister's house. Susan's family were delightful, all of them, their cat and two dogs included. Her daughter Sally was three and was at home during the afternoons, the twins were older and would be in school now. True, the household was sometimes chaotic but it was also filled with love. It was a place where they could all be themselves, without pretences or veneers, which was, to Becky's way of thinking, something precious. Surely Susan thought so too, deep down inside?

'Rebecca? The cat lives, you'll be glad to know. Now where was I? Oh, yes, you and your lovely lifestyle. You don't know when you're well off. The world is your oyster, you're earning pots of money, you've got clothes, looks, admirers and—bother!...Sally, don't *do* that! Cats don't like that, darling, they really don't! Now put her down, at once! Sorry, Rebecca. You see what I mean about knowing when you're well off?'

'And you're not, I suppose? Is that what you're telling me?'

'Well, no, not exactly——'

'Susan, I've got no time for this conversation just now. And in any case you're only paying lip service——'

'Lip service!' Her sister almost screeched her protest. 'Lip service? I'm pointing out that you should count your blessings.'

Becky answered that softly in an effort to hide her irritation. 'And you yours.'

There was a momentary silence before: 'I do, Rebecca. I've taken your point. It's a case of the other man's grass, isn't it?'

'Something like that. Listen, what I really wanted to tell you was—well, you'll never guess who was on the flight from New York.'

'OK, I'll never guess, so tell me.'

'Stirling Robard.'

'Who?'

'You can't have forgotten him! Stirling Robard——'

There was laughter, giggles that made Susan sound younger than her thirty years. 'Forgotten him? No way! Good heavens, I used to be halfway in love with the man! Is he still as dishy? No, I'll bet he's dishier now he's older. Are you seeing him again? Did you make a date with him?'

'No, Susan, I did not. You and Ian might have thought him marvellous but I never did. I thought him extremely insensitive, and I've got news for you—he hasn't changed a bit.'

There was a silence, then a sigh. 'You always were a touchy child, Rebecca. And at moments like this I think you haven't changed, either.'

The conversation was over as far as Becky was concerned. What was the point in it? 'Susan, my money's about to run out. Take care, give my love to the family and I'll be in touch.'

It was during the flight to Zurich that Becky began to yearn for the comfort of a soft bed. It was a small plane compared to the one she had taken from New York— there was no room to stretch out and her legs were feeling cramped. They were long legs, too. Sometimes she got called 'Legs' rather than Becky—by photographers mostly, the male variety of course. It was only her family who called her Rebecca.

She thought back to her telephone call to her sister. It had depressed her vaguely, although she couldn't quite pinpoint why. She shifted in her seat, trying to be honest with herself. Stirling had been right in saying her parents had spoiled her. They had; they had doted on her and they still did. As far as they, and Ian and Susan, were concerned, she had been very much 'the baby'—and maybe that had been the trouble. Even when she had shown signs of growing up, they hadn't treated her any differently. As far as she could remember, nobody had taken her seriously in any way—except Stirling Robard.

Now, she looked down at fluffy white clouds and admitted that there had been a certain satisfaction in his seeing her as she looked these days, not that he had been impressed. Oh, he had said she was tall and slim and beautiful but he had not looked at her as other men looked at her—not that she had wanted him to—and when she'd told him she was a model, he had looked at her with distaste. Hadn't he? Or had she imagined that?

Feeling exhausted, she closed her eyes and thought ahead: of meeting Ingrid at the airport, of exchanging news and laughter, and she began to perk up. A friend of Michael McCaffrey had said she still had a lot of living to do. She decided he was right. A few days' rest and she would be ready for fun, more fun. The world was her oyster, as Susan had said, and she was going to make the most of things. And why not? Unless and until the time came when she wanted to settle down, she was going to live it up at every given opportunity.

An hour later she was being hugged by Ingrid on the other side of the Customs barrier in Zurich airport. 'Ingrid, I'm going to love it here. This airport is something else, *everything* is automated and it's so *clean*!'

They started laughing, setting the mood for the rest of the day. 'You think you're going to like my little country? Just because you like the airport? Becky, you're crazy! You're right but you're crazy. Now, how was your flight, I mean your flights, any problems?'

'Apart from a delayed take-off in New York, none at all.' Becky shrugged, following Ingrid in the direction of the exit. She wasn't going to mention Stirling Robard. The name wouldn't mean anything to her friend and in any case it was water under the bridge, all of it—today's meeting and the experiences ten years ago. The whole thing was as good as forgotten.

'Super. And what of New York? How did you get on with Michael McCaffrey? That was his name, wasn't it?'

Ingrid hadn't met Michael, she had only learned of his existence during a phone call from Becky. Ingrid had left Los Angeles in the morning and Becky had been introduced to Michael there during the evening, in a nightclub the gang had gone to to celebrate the end of their assignment. They had all been due to fly back to London together the next day—but Becky had got on very well with Michael and, reassured by the photographer who had introduced them that Michael was crazy but respectable, had accepted his invitation to spend a few days at his apartment in New York.

'Yes, and he's delightful, a great sense of humour and a lot of fun. A bit wild but I liked him, I liked him a lot.'

'What does that mean? Did you have an affair with him?' It was not a serious question; Ingrid knew her friend better than that. She ought to—they had lived together for over three years. 'Come on, Becky, you just told me you had a lot of fun—what kind of fun?'

'Not that kind. I wasn't his only house-guest. I was sharing a bedroom with another girl, another *platonic* friend of Michael's. Now don't start winding me up, I'm too tired for that kind of teasing.'

The other girl threw up her arms, looking heavenwards. 'I don't know what I'm going to do with you, I can't decide whether you're afraid of sex or not. I'm serious, you know. I've lost count of the number of men you've been out with—and you claim there's something wrong with all of them. What are you looking for, perfection? You'll never find it. I think you are afraid.'

'You can think what you like, dear heart. I've told you before, jumping into bed with a man is not something I could do just like that.'

'You mean just like me.'

'I didn't say that, Ingrid. And face it, these days——'

'What? What's the matter?'

Rebecca was looking at the sleek black Jaguar parked right outside the airport doors, gleaming in the fading sunlight. It wasn't the car that surprised her, it was the chauffeur who went with it. He was tipping his hat, reaching for the cases on her trolley. In a low mutter she said, 'Ingrid, what haven't you told me?'

'About what?'

'About the fact that you go around in a chauffeur-driven car.'

There was a shrug, a laugh. 'You know my father's well off.'

Rebecca had known that; she knew Ingrid got an allowance from her father regardless of her own high earnings. She knew he was some kind of investment manager—or something—but that was all. '*How* well off?' she asked with a grin.

'*Very* well off,' said Ingrid, grinning just as broadly and looking quite angelic. 'So aren't I the lucky girl?'

They climbed into the car and picked up where they'd left off. Ingrid wanted to know more about Michael McCaffrey. 'Are you likely to see him again? What was he doing in Los Angeles? Does he ever get to England? What does he look like?'

'You set too much store by looks, Ingrid, I've told you that before. I'm more interested in character than in looks. The looks of a person, no matter how attractive they might appear, are no indication——'

'Aw, Becky! Don't lecture me, just tell me!'

They started laughing again. They were in many ways a good foil for one another, the blonde and the brunette—they were very close but very different. They had never fought but there had been many heated discussions between them. It made life interesting, though, and despite all this Ingrid was very easy to live with. 'OK, Michael is not what *you* would call a looker. He is, however, interesting and, as I said, a bit wild. He's an artist and——'

'Ah! Possibly of dubious sexual inclination then.'

'I doubt it. He asked me to marry him.'

Ingrid looked aghast. 'He can't have been serious!'

'Thank you, friend. He was. I know,' Becky added, laughing again, 'and I'll say it first, it takes all sorts. Michael is eccentric to say the least. You wouldn't believe what his apartment was like.'

'Fantastic?'

'Scruffy. As eccentric as he. Lots of nice stuff going to ruin. He seems to think life is one long party and——'

'You mean it isn't?'

'And I don't know how he manages to get any work done, to *produce* anything. But he's——' Becky broke off to look out of the window for a moment. Zurich, from what she could see of it, was not particularly impressive. 'He's delightful.'

'So might you see him again?'

'I shouldn't think so—he divides his time between Los Angeles and New York and I've no idea whether he ever goes to England—or whether I'd see him if he did. Now that's enough about me. What about you? How are your parents?'

'Exactly the same,' Ingrid said, which was not very informative. 'I mean, you know... They're a good pair, there's never any problem with them—except for their complaints that I don't come home often enough.'

'Well, it has been ages and you are their only child.'

'Mm. Anyway, things will be a bit different soon, I mean Daddy will be making trips to London quite frequently from now on and I'm sure Mummy will come with him—if only for the shopping. A few months ago he sold his business to another company, a bigger organisation that has branches in New York, Paris and London as well as Zurich and Berne. He doesn't need to work at all, of course, but he enjoys it and he's acting as a consultant to the company now. I have to confess that he is brilliant where money is concerned—at least, I suppose he is! Personally I find talk of investments and heaven knows what very boring. I don't encourage my father to talk about his work—I advise you to do the same. Otherwise he'll go on and on, believe me! Which reminds me,' she added apologetically. 'At the party on Saturday, there'll be a lot of it. It's inevitable.'

'You've lost me, Ingrid. A lot of what?'

'My father's kind of mumbo-jumbo.'

Becky was frowning and smiling at the same time. Ingrid's mother tongue was Schweizer-Deutsch and she did speak with an accent—but her command of English left nothing to be desired. 'Mumbo-jumbo?'

'Money talk. My father's friends, colleagues. I mean there'll be a lot of them at the anniversary party.'

'Oh, I see. Well, naturally. That won't worry me.' Becky was looking out of the window again. The scenery had changed completely and it was, she thought, absolutely beautiful. Charming Swiss chalets, mountains and forests were all around her now. She was glad she had come at this time of year; she had never seen so many trees, so many shades of autumn.

'I begin to see what people rave about,' she told Ingrid.

'Wait till you see Lake Lucerne,' came the quiet reply.

Becky turned to smile at her friend, at the unmistakable pride in her voice. Ingrid might choose not to live in Switzerland but she was very proud of her country, that was for certain.

It took only forty-five minutes to drive from Zurich to Lucerne and when Rebecca first glimpsed the lake she understood more and more. It was far bigger than she had imagined and it was stunning. Across the water mountains towered majestically, their peaks glinting in the setting sun. And then, momentarily, the lake was out of sight as the car turned off and began to climb along a twisting road. When next she looked the lake was even prettier: she could see a steamer cutting along it, sailboats dotted here and there. It was shimmering silver-red now, clear and cool and inviting. She could hardly wait to sail on it, to trail her fingers in the water.

'We're being very lucky with the weather,' Ingrid said, enjoying Becky's admiration. 'It's been like midsummer these past few days and they say it's going to continue for at least a week.'

Becky's thoughts flitted to the contents of her suitcases. All contingencies were covered, apart from shoes; she had plenty of everything else from evening wear to swimwear. In any case she could buy whatever else she might need; the shopping in Lucerne was good, according to Ingrid.

Her next surprise was Ingrid's home. It was not the typical Swiss-chalet style but a low, modern villa painted white. It was deceptive in size—it was far bigger than it appeared to be—and the view it commanded of the lake was superb. After introductions had been made, Ingrid, her parents and a maid accompanied Becky to her room. Inwardly amused, she answered their questions and stood on the veranda, absorbing the view. Their welcome was so warm and friendly that she was very touched. Was the room to her liking? Would she enjoy the view? Had she had something to eat? Would she like something to eat?

She turned to them, her arms sweeping towards the lake. 'Everything, but everything, is perfect! I'm going to have a wonderful time, thank you so much. It's gorgeous, all of it. And no, honestly, there's nothing I want now except a cup of tea.'

'Ah!' Ingrid's father clapped his hands together. Bruno Bachmann was stocky and squat, some six inches shorter than his wife, Isabelle. They were both charming, Becky thought, liking the way they smiled so readily. 'Then come, Becky, and we will all have tea in the big room.'

It was an accurate description; the big room was big and it overlooked the lake. Again, its furnishings were not typically Swiss but they were luxurious. Becky sat on one of three white settees and drank three cups of tea, refusing very firmly the pastries set out on a low coffee-table, although it wasn't an easy thing to do.

'You girls,' said Ingrid's mother, 'are too thin. Men do not like that, this thinness. You should think of this.'

'We do all right,' Ingrid put in mischievously, while Becky simultaneously said,

'In our work, slimness is necessary.'

'You see, Isabelle!' Ingrid's father shook his head as if all were hopeless. 'With the younger generation one gets nowhere. They know it all.'

The girls laughed, knowing he wasn't serious, and for the following hour they all chatted and got to know one another better. By the time dinner was over that evening, Becky felt perfectly at ease with Bruno and Isabelle Bachmann—and happy with the world in general. After a brief walk with Ingrid, she went to bed and slept for twelve solid hours.

For the next few days Rebecca slept late and re-charged her batteries, then, having adjusted to the time difference, she set about the serious business of shopping with her friend.

'Are you enjoying yourself?' Ingrid asked unnecess-arily. They had stopped for lunch in an open-air café in the old section of Lucerne and Becky's face was turned up to the sun while they dawdled over coffee.

She fished in her bag for her dark glasses and laughed delightedly. 'I'm loving it. I can't believe you'd ever want to leave this place.'

'I'll come back to stay one day. In the meantime, it's—well, it's too constricting. Too small and limiting for me.'

'I could live here happily ever after.'

'Oh, yes? You've only been here four days. Wait and see. Come on, if you want new shoes for the party tomorrow, let's get a move on. I know what you're like when it comes to buying shoes...'

The days had sped by. It was Friday already. According to Ingrid, some other house-guests would arrive that evening. 'There are three of them coming this evening, Daddy's director-general and a married couple who live in France—they've been friends of my parents since before I was born.'

Becky took off her glasses—clouds were sneaking across the sun. 'I hope they all speak English?'

'Yes, of course.'

Of course. Virtually all the Swiss spoke some English, and some French and Italian and German. To them it was essential, living in such a small country, surrounded as they were by the other countries. 'The English,' she said, 'are very lazy when it comes to learning other languages.'

'Very lazy,' Ingrid agreed. 'Speaking of which, come on, move yourself. We're in for a shower by the look of it.'

They were. Within half an hour it was raining and they were walking around with no protection. Neither of them minded. They went from shoe shop to shoe shop undaunted—until Ingrid started shivering. By then it was almost four o'clock and it had chilled off considerably.

They took a taxi back to the villa, very damp but feeling quite pleased with themselves—or rather with the contents of their respective carrier bags. 'Hey, look at *that*! Gorgeous, isn't it?' Rebecca followed Ingrid's admiring gaze and looked at the white Rolls-Royce Corniche parked at the back of the villa, asking who it belonged to.

'I don't know, but it has Swiss number-plates.'

Ingrid paid the taxi-driver and they gathered all their bags together and dumped the lot in the hall, going straight through to the living-room to let Isabelle and Bruno know they were home...at which point Becky suddenly wished herself elsewhere.

There was only one person in the living-room and he was standing with his back to them, looking out across the lake, his hands thrust deep into the pockets of his trousers. Ingrid and Becky exchanged looks and Ingrid shrugged. She had no idea who the man was.

But Becky knew him. She knew, before he turned around to face them, that the figure by the window was Stirling Robard.

She blinked in disbelief, a small gasp escaping from her as she felt rather than saw Ingrid's swift look, knowing it would be one of puzzlement. She left it to Ingrid to address the man because she herself couldn't say anything, she was too stunned for words.

It was he who spoke first, however. He turned, smiling, his slate-grey eyes taking in both girls before he inclined his head politely and crossed the room. 'Ladies, how very nice this is! You must be Ingrid,' he added, holding out his hand to her. 'Your father has shown me several photographs of you. He's very proud of you, being a model, you know.'

Becky had never seen her friend behave so shyly. She seemed oddly bereft of her usual confidence, answering in something that came close to a stammer. 'He is? I— well, I hope he is. A-and you are...?'

'Stirling Robard.'

'Oh! Well, I...er, excuse me.' She turned away quickly, sneezing. 'Excuse me,' she repeated lamely, looking lost in her own living-room. 'Umm, Becky, let me introduce you to the director-general of——'

'An introduction won't be necessary,' Stirling cut in quietly, his grey eyes on Becky's, mocking, filled with silent laughter. 'Rebecca, how... interesting it is to see you again. How are you?'

She found her voice. It was more than she could do to smile but she could at least speak now. 'The same as I was a few days ago. Go on, laugh if you must.' And he did, just as he had laughed at Heathrow Airport— laughter which she now understood. 'This is all a big joke to you, isn't it?'

'Very much so,' he agreed smoothly, ignoring Ingrid's increasing curiosity. 'And to you it's not funny at all, is it? As I said, you still have no sense of humour...'

CHAPTER THREE

'I CAN'T believe it.' Ingrid was looking at Becky wide-eyed, shaking her head. 'I mean, he's so *attractive*! I wish my father had told me more about him. All I'd heard was his name and Daddy's insistence that the new director-general is, I quote, a financial genius. I'd taken it for granted he would be much older and I'd assumed he was American. He's just my type, Becky, tall, broad—and fantastic eyes, don't you think? I just can't believe it!'

They had both spent an hour over tea with her parents and Stirling, listening but saying little. In different ways they had both been stunned by his presence at the villa but, while Ingrid was delighted by it, Becky was not.

'You can't believe it? Can you imagine how I feel?' They were in Ingrid's bathroom. Becky was sitting on a linen basket, her feet propped on the lavatory, whilst her friend soaked luxuriously in a bubble bath. It was the first chance they'd had to talk in private since they'd got home. 'My tranquillity is shot to pieces.'

'Oh, Becky, don't be like that. He seemed OK to me, more than OK!'

'How many times do I have to tell you? You can't judge a book by looking at its cover.'

'He's got character, my friend. You can see it in his eyes.'

'Oh, yes,' Becky drawled, 'he's got character all right. The trouble is I don't like it—and neither will you. I've just given you the run-down on my experience of him but you don't seem to believe me.'

'Of course I believe you. But your having a crush on him must have made things worse than they were. In any case, you were probably hypersensitive as a child, because of all your problems.'

Becky paused before answering. Hypersensitive? Well, perhaps she had been. 'You're probably right. But he's totally *insensitive*, Ingrid. He's also as hard as nails, obviously world-weary and as cynical as they make them. That's what *I* see in his eyes. I can't tell you whether it was always there, I suspect it's happened to him during the past ten years—on his way up the ladder of success.'

'Now who's being cynical? What's wrong with success?'

'Nothing. Good luck to him. I mean it. Financial genius or not, he must have worked very hard to get where he is.'

'How old is he, exactly?'

Becky thought for a moment. Ian was thirty-one, almost thirty-two. 'He's probably thirty-four or -five. I know he started university late because he had problems with his parents, or a parent. Or something.'

Ingrid lifted a leg from the water, considered it and let it dangle over the side of the bath. 'He's got a house here.'

'What? Who has?'

'Who are we talking about? Our Mr Robard, of course. I remember my father telling me he's got a house in Stans, or just outside Stans. It's across the lake, not far from here.'

'But—but why is he staying here then? I mean—here.'

'I know what you mean,' Ingrid grinned. 'And do stop spluttering, Becky! Stirling's house is being decorated so he's staying here for a few days until it's finished, that's all.'

'That's all?' Relieved, Rebecca got to her feet. 'Well, I'm very glad to hear it.'

'Where are you going?'

'To my room, to get ready for dinner. You'd better get a move on, too, if we're all gathering for drinks at eight o'clock.'

It had been the same pleasant ritual every evening so far: the Bachmanns dressed for dinner and they took drinks in the living-room first. Tonight would be different; tonight there would be three extra guests with the Bachmanns' old friends, the couple who lived in France. They had arrived just as Becky and Ingrid had been making their escape earlier. At least they had seemed pleasant enough.

After a quick shower Becky made up lightly and put on a simple black cocktail dress which did wonders for her suntan. With practised ease she gathered her dark hair on to her crown, twisted it and pinned it into a knot, leaving a few loose tendrils to soften the style. She clipped on plain silver earrings with a matching necklace and her silver watch—and that was it. It had been no effort but the overall effect was good, very good. She surveyed herself in the full-length mirror on the bathroom door and nodded in satisfaction.

'Ready?' Ingrid walked in without knocking, her eyes narrowing as she took in Becky's appearance. 'You've gone to a lot of trouble tonight.'

'What do you mean?'

'I mean for someone who claims to be uninterested in our rich and handsome house-guest, you've gone to a lot of trouble.'

Becky couldn't even smile. The situation was not, in her opinion, the joke Stirling Robard seemed to think it. And now Ingrid was behaving as if it were amusing, too. 'On the contrary,' she said crossly. 'It's all thanks to the dress.'

'It's all thanks to the figure underneath it.'

It was Rebecca's turn to survey Ingrid. 'You don't look too bad yourself.' She held up a hand. 'And don't bother to deny it, it's patently obvious *you* are out to make an impression.'

'Who's denying it?' came the laughing reply.

They were both complimented when they walked into the living-room—by Ingrid's parents and by their friends. Stirling had not yet put in an appearance. When he did, all eyes turned to him and Isabelle Bachmann took his arm.

'Come, Stirling, and tell us what you will drink. Ahh, but you look magnificent! What do you say, Ingrid?'

Becky looked away, determined not to be drawn into this. The fact that he did look magnificent was beside the point. Even she had to admit to his attractiveness now. Well over six feet tall, Stirling Robard had a superb physique, with wide shoulders and chest tapering to slim hips. He was broader, more solid than she remembered him from years ago but he was every bit as fit. His blond hair was darker than usual—still damp from the shower, no doubt. It was cut neat and short but not too short, detracting in no way from the strong, chiselled features of his face. He was wearing a white evening jacket with black trousers...and there was no denying that he looked good. It was just a pity, Becky thought, that he didn't have the inner qualities which she deemed to be far more important.

It was not Ingrid's style to fawn over a man but Becky didn't even want to hear her reply. Her mother had put her on the spot and she would have to say something complimentary. Stirling was, after all, Bruno Bachmann's boss.

Fortunately there were enough people present to enable Becky to avoid the Englishman. She chatted with the old friends of her hosts, and with Bruno, and managed nicely to say no more than good evening to Stirling. She thought she had handled it all without being impolite—until she was informed to the contrary.

Suddenly Ingrid was at her side, whispering harshly, 'What's the matter with you? You're not going to create an atmosphere, are you? Can't you at least be civil to him?'

'I'm—I haven't——'

'Yes, you have. Daddy's wondering about it already. Do make an effort, Becky. Please!'

She felt guilty. Ingrid looked genuinely perturbed. Happily it didn't last long, any of it, her guilt or her friend's discomfort. Stirling walked over to them and proffered both arms when it was time to go and eat.

'Ladies,' he said, with that characteristic inclination of his head, 'it seems I have the pleasure of escorting you both in to dinner.'

Becky put on a smile, her eyes flitting briefly to her friend as they both slipped an arm through Stirling's. She had, she knew, better behave herself, even if this physical contact with him was unwanted. It was, she mused, odd that his touch could affect her so after all these years, odd that she felt so strongly inclined to pull away from him.

With the Bachmanns in front and the other couple behind, they all walked in to the dining-room where, to

Becky's regret, Isabelle put Stirling next to her. As he saw her seated first, he leaned down and managed with a few words to wipe the smile from her face. 'And a dubious pleasure it was. Loosen up, Rebecca, you're being a drag.'

She ignored the remark, turning instead to the man on her left, who was only too happy to be the object of her attention. 'So, Benedikt, what made you leave Switzerland to go and live in France? I take it you and your wife have been there for some years?'

Until they were halfway through the main course, there were several conversations taking place. Stirling's attention was on Isabelle, who was sitting on his right, and for the time being all was well. It was during dessert that there was a lull, which Isabelle broke by talking about Saturday.

'And what about tomorrow?' she asked the room at large. 'Benedikt, you and Heidi are going to visit your mother in Zurich, aren't you?'

They were, they said, but they would be back well in time for the start of the party.

'And you, Stirling? You will be talking business with Bruno in his study, I suppose?'

'Certainly not.' He looked from his host to his hostess with a smile. 'In this weather? What a waste! No, I thought I'd take the girls out for a drive. The three of us could have lunch together in——'

'Not I,' Ingrid said, her blonde curls shimmering around her as she gently shook her head. 'Thank you for the thought, but I want to stay here to help my mother. She'll deny it, but I know she'll be in a flap tomorrow.'

Isabelle wanted to know the meaning of the word 'flap'. 'It means you'll need me, Mummy, in spite of your well-trained staff and whoever else you've organised to do things. I shall be staying home to organise the organiser—and no arguments.' She looked back at Stirling, deliberately avoiding Becky's eyes as she gave him her most angelic smile. 'But that needn't spoil your plans, Stirling. I'm sure Becky will be very grateful if you'll show her some sights. Do you know, she hasn't even been up a mountain yet, all she's seen is the town.'

There was the slightest hesitation, one that nobody else noticed, before he said, 'Is that so?' Then he turned to Rebecca, his eyes belying the smile on his mouth. 'That must be rectified, of course. In which case we'll have lunch on a mountain and we'll do some sight-seeing.'

Becky had no intention of having lunch on a mountain—with him. Not that she demurred right now; it was more than she dared do because all eyes were on her. 'I'll look forward to it,' she said politely.

'Good, good!' Isabelle was delighted. 'And you can catch up on the many years of news you have.' At Rebecca's look, she explained, 'Stirling told us earlier that you and he knew each other years ago, Becky, that you are old friends. It is an odd thing, your meeting again like this, here, isn't it?'

'Very odd,' Becky said drily.

She got up at eight the following morning. One look at the sky told her it was going to be another beautiful day. Jeans and a T-shirt would do. She went down to breakfast and found everyone on the patio, eating—albeit at different stages. Ingrid was having her usual cup of coffee and nothing else. Stirling was tucking into three eggs, German sausages and what looked like fried potatoes. Becky couldn't help smiling; there was enough food on his breakfast plate to keep her going for two days.

He caught the amusement in her eyes as she sat opposite him. 'Good morning, Rebecca. Sleep well?'

'Very.' She glanced away, wishing she hadn't noticed how much his smile softened his features, how it softened the colour of his eyes, wishing she were not so acutely aware of his presence. It seemed to dominate somehow; it had been the same at dinner the previous evening. Even when she hadn't been looking at him, she had been aware of him.

A little later he suggested they start their day. 'When you're ready, Rebecca. You'll need a warm sweater, you'll find it cold on the mountain. Did you bring a heavy sweater with you?'

She had, and she didn't argue. The easiest thing would be to fetch a sweater from her room—not that she would need it. She was back in less than two minutes. 'I'm ready.'

They said goodbye to everyone and she walked around the villa with him to his car, slipping gracefully into the plush, red leather passenger seat whilst he held the door open for her. The hood of the Corniche was down, its beautiful white paintwork was gleaming in the early sunshine, and Becky half regretted what she was about to do. It would, she conceded, have been a pleasure to ride around in the luxury of this car all day—with different company. She flung her bag and her sweater on the back seat and waited for Stirling to get in.

'You can drop me in town,' she said without preamble.

'What?'

'You heard me, Stirling. You didn't really think I'd want to spend an entire day with you, did you?'

He wasn't amused this time, far from it. 'What the hell are you talking about?'

'I'm talking about you and me going sight-seeing, having lunch and all that. How very civilised—but no, thanks.'

He had not yet switched the engine on; his hands were on the wheel and he was facing her. Indeed, he was staring at her. 'Now let me get this straight. All that, last night and this morning, was a pretence, for the benefit of the others. Right?'

'Right. No one will know we've gone our separate ways. We'll meet in town later and drive back here together.'

In a voice that was not like his own, he said, 'I don't believe this.'

'Believe it,' she said coolly. 'I have no wish to go out with you, today or any other day.' She met his scrutiny and noted from the corner of her eye that his fingers had curled around the steering wheel. Had she managed to crack his composure at last?

She hadn't. He just smiled, switched the engine on and started to reverse the car.

'I'm serious, Stirling, I want to be *alone*.'

'You and Greta Garbo.'

'Stirling——'

He had turned on to the main road, driving faster than was necessary, causing her to shift in her seat. 'Belt up,' he said, and she did; the safety harness was already in her hand when he went on. 'I'm going to give you a chance, so make the most of it.'

For seconds Becky was stuck for words. 'A chance to what?'

'To find out what a very nice person I am. To stop associating me with—whatever you've got fixed in your memory from the past.'

If she had wanted to smile at the first part of his answer, it quickly passed because his second statement made her think. Perhaps he was right. She did equate him with the past, with a lack of understanding and sensitivity. Maybe, just maybe, he was different now.

'I'm different,' he went on, as if he'd read her thoughts. 'But that is not meant as an apology, because in fact I never did or said anything that was detrimental to you. And surely you've changed in the past ten years? In some respects, at least?'

She glanced away, acknowledging that perhaps she was being childish again. Of course she had changed in the past ten years, inside as well as outside, enormously. 'All right,' she said at length. 'We'll have lunch together.'

He said nothing, and she noticed that in any case they were turning on to a freeway now, heading in quite the wrong direction for the town of Lucerne. She folded her arms, her long hair flying in the breeze as they sped along, realising that he'd had no intention of dropping her in the town. 'But I don't know why you're bothering,' she added, 'because in truth you don't want to be alone with me any more than I want to be with you. That was obvious from the way you hesitated last night.'

He didn't comment, he merely glanced at her and changed the subject. 'There's a headscarf in that locker. You'd better put it on if you hope to get a comb through your hair later.'

A headscarf! she thought, unable to control her cynicism. He was probably a womaniser, he certainly had the looks—and everything else to go with it. No doubt he kept scarves handy for his lady passengers—he probably had dozens of them, women-friends whom he took out to impress in a car that cost more money than the house she had been brought up in. Well, she wasn't impressed . . . but she couldn't deny a certain curiosity. There was very little she could recall about Stirling's family, his background, but she did know that he had not come from a wealthy family. She sneaked a look at him, at the strong, fine profile, and wondered what his life had been like since he had left university.

For over half an hour they drove in silence and for most of the time Becky forgot who she was with because the scenery was so breathtaking. She had eyes for nothing else. They were driving higher and higher around a gently curving road, not too fast now, moving at a pace which allowed her to see everything. They drove through forests, they passed lakes and streams and met with very little traffic. The sun was shimmering down from a pure blue sky and in the near distance she could hear the tinkle of cow-bells and the rattle of the funicular railway— something she had yet to experience. It was idyllic, the greenery so very lush and rich, and once again she marvelled at Ingrid's being able to live in London when there was all this beauty in her own country, right on her own doorstep.

'Better?' Stirling asked suddenly, startling her.

'I'm—what do you mean?'

'Your mood, Rebecca. I was hoping the peacefulness would have got to you. Seems to me you haven't wound down from your escapades yet.'

She looked at him, genuinely sorry that he had managed to say the wrong thing. Escapades? What was that supposed to mean? 'Are you referring to the work I was doing in Los Angeles?'

'You call modelling work, do you?'

Irritated, she turned away again. What would he know?

'Well, Rebecca? What made you go in for modelling, of all things?'

'Get off my back, Stirling.'

'There was a time,' he said, 'when I was impressed by beauty. By beautiful women, I mean. There was a time when I would have been impressed by your beauty, very much so. Fortunately I grew up.'

She didn't rise to it—she let his words blow away on the wind.

'That was a compliment, Rebecca. Or are you still so set against me that you couldn't hear it?'

She sighed. 'I heard. You said you were once impressed by beauty but it now leaves you cold.'

Stirling's laughter was sudden and soft, drawing her eyes to him. 'Don't put words in my mouth. What I'm saying is that I realised how irrelevant it is. What matters is what's in here,' he added, touching his temple, 'and most especially in here...' and then his heart.

Becky might have commented in complete agreement had they still been on the road, but they weren't; they had just turned off and were driving on to a car park. It was the station where one took the cable-car and she turned to him in surprise. 'We're going on a cable-car?'

'Three, actually. Unless you're about to make a run for it. How else do we climb a ten-thousand-foot mountain?'

Ten thousand feet! 'I'm—not sure I want to!'

'Not sure you want to run away?'

'No, I'm not sure I want to go in one cable-car, let alone three.'

'You've never been in one?'

'Well, yes—but not like those! And I only did it because it was necessary. I went skiing and——'

'So what's the problem?'

Becky was looking up at the mountain. She could see the little cars sailing up the side of it as if determined in their quest. From where she sat they seemed to be travelling vertically and they were only tiny capsules, tiny yellow things much smaller than the one she had been on in Italy. 'I loathed it.'

'The skiing?'

Clicking her tongue, she dragged her eyes away from the cable cars and turned to him. She was about to ask him why he seemed insistent on misunderstanding her, but it didn't work out like that. Instead she caught him silently laughing, and for a moment she couldn't speak at all. His eyes were so—different, again. She glimpsed the genuine humour in them and . . . and the softness she had seen at breakfast. Mentally she shook herself, telling herself it had to be a trick of the light, the now brilliant sunlight. 'You're laughing at me.'

'No, just teasing you.' And still his eyes were soft as they looked into hers. 'Do you mind?'

'No, I suppose not.' Nor could she prevent herself from smiling.

'Good. Come on, then, I told you we'd have lunch on a mountain and that's precisely what we're going to do. I thought this one would be the best. Its name is Titlis, it has a glacier and it's the biggest around here. It isn't the prettiest but in my opinion it's the most interesting. Wait till you see the views!'

His enthusiasm was contagious and ten minutes later they were stepping into a small cable-car which was no bigger than a bubble to Becky's eyes. Her heart was in her throat, excitement and fear battling for precedence inside her. She tried to act casually but she would have given anything for a little comfort, to have had a hand to hold. There were just the two of them in the car and she sat opposite Stirling, crossing her arms and her legs as she did so.

He patted the seat next to him. 'If you sat here, you could see where you're going rather than where you've been.'

'I'm fine.'

'There'd be another advantage, too.'

'Namely?'

'You could hold my hand.'

He grinned and she turned to look out of the window—just as the car lurched into motion and began its ascent. Involuntarily her eyes closed.

'Rebecca? Are you all right?'

'I told you, I'm...fine.' It was more than she could do to open her eyes, and she had heard the tremor in her voice. If he laughs now, she thought, I shall hate him for ever and a day.

He didn't laugh. He warned her that he was about to change seats and she should not be alarmed.

Becky was alarmed—the car rocked on its cable and it shocked her, but the feel of Stirling's arm coming around her was even more shocking. It was meant as a protective gesture, of course, a comforting one, but she started as if she had been threatened by something dangerous.

'Take it easy,' he said. 'Have you any idea how safe these things are?'

'Tell me about it.' It was something to say, and maybe it would distract her from the scent of him, the feel of him, which was indeed threatening as well as comforting.

Stirling did just that, in fact he gave her a lecture on the principles of their working and he did a good re-assurance job on her. By the time they reached the station where they disembarked to take the next car, she was feeling more confident—and grateful that he was no longer touching her. 'The Swiss are extremely conscientious when it comes to safety, you know. Even the private boats you'll see on the lake have to be checked regularly for safety...'

Rebecca climbed into the next car, her stomach somewhat steadier, but she made no protest when Stirling sat next to her. The ground was a long way below her and the panorama around them, stunning though it was, was at an angle that was making her dizzy. She was still a little frightened.

Up ahead she could see the glacier, cold and grey and distant—an exact description of the way she had seen Stirling's eyes all too recently. Wrongly, though. At least, that was not the way she saw them now. He was looking at her now with unmistakable concern, asking again whether she was feeling all right.

She assured him she was, and, miraculously, it was true.

When they got to the platform to wait for their third and last car, he smiled and took hold of the sweater she had draped over her arm. 'It might be a good idea to put this round your shoulders.' After a thoughtful pause he added, 'And, if you're agreeable, we could perhaps begin all over again.'

Rebecca was standing two feet from him, finding herself quite fascinated by the glint of the sun on his hair. It was making it blonder than ever and in those few seconds she thought him beautiful. 'I—what did you say?'

'I said we could begin again, Rebecca. We could start our day all over again, without any cross words or reluctance having been in the way.'

Had he not turned away from her, she might have laughed at the idea. As it was, she found herself looking at the nape of his neck and feeling the sudden, ludicrous urge to touch him there, just where his hair finished and curled slightly. It took an effort to drag her mind back to what he'd just said. 'That's a good idea but I think I can improve on it.'

'I'm listening.' He turned to look at her and she almost lost courage.

Almost, but not quite. 'We could pretend we've just met, here, for the first time, and start again. We could pretend that we're meeting for the first time ever, that we know nothing at all about each other. After all, we don't really know much, do we?'

He smiled, conveying agreement that indeed they knew very little about one another.

Becky began the game first, holding out her hand to him. 'My name is Rebecca Hill, and you are...?'

'Stirling Robard.' He shook her hand firmly, glancing over her shoulder as he did so. 'The car's coming. Well, Rebecca Hill, since we both appear to be alone, when we get to the restaurant perhaps you'll have lunch with me?'

'That would be very pleasant.' She turned, smiling to herself, and saw that the final cable-car was red and much bigger than the ones they'd been on so far. One could stand up in it, which she did, holding on to a rail with Stirling just a few feet away from her. Slowly, the car inched its way along the cable at an impossible angle and for minutes Becky forgot the game, forgot everything as she gazed around in awe at the gigantic glacier.

She jumped at the sudden sound of Stirling's voice. 'Makes you feel insignificant, doesn't it?'

'It does. It's...it's just incredible. I love it, but I think I could use a drink. How about it, before we have lunch?'

He inclined his head, doing his best to suppress his amusement. 'We can do that outdoors, on the sun terrace.'

For the moment the sky was perfectly clear immediately above them, but below them were patches of swirling cloud. Becky put on her sweater properly because it was chilly in spite of the sunshine.

When they were seated at a table with a couple of drinks, they continued their game, which proved to be very enjoyable at first.

'...and then I left school and I worked in an office for a while. But I soon got bored with that, so I trained to be a model. That's what I've been doing for the past four years, though there was a time when one would have thought it the last thing I'd do for a living.'

'Really? Why is that?'

'I used to look the very antithesis of what a model's supposed to look like.'

Stirling let his eyes trail over her, over her face, her hair—and then over what he could see of her body. 'Unbelievable,' he said, bringing his eyes back to hers. 'I find that really difficult to believe.'

'Well, take my word. I was very fat as a youngster.'

He smiled. 'But you always had a lovely face, Rebecca...'

She wagged a finger at him. 'You're cheating!'

'Oh. Yes. Just forgot myself for a moment.'

'Come on, it's your turn. What about you?'

He gave her a run-down of his very early life, telling her he was an only child and that he had been born in Oxford. It was when he mentioned the death of his mother that Becky, in turn, forgot the game. 'My mother was killed riding a bike when I was nine——'

'Stirling, I had no idea! I didn't recall that your mother had died, and when you were so young...'

He smiled, reaching to put a finger to her lips. He didn't quite touch her—he stopped within an inch of her mouth, going on, 'And after her death, my father, who was very bright and who earned a lot of money, proceeded to drink himself slowly to death. He lost his desire to live and in time he lost his job. He took some years to kill himself and I looked after him as best I could, but he got worse. Eventually he——'

Again Becky broke the rules. She gasped. She had known he had had a problem during his university years but she hadn't known exactly what it was. She shook her head. 'Sorry. Go on.'

'Eventually he went into a home where they tried to dry him out, and that was a pattern which repeated itself for a few years. Then the time came when it was too late even to hope and—he died.' He broke off, glancing away, and for long seconds she thought he would not continue. He seemed to be struggling inwardly, although there was very little emotion showing on his face.

Briefly, Becky's eyes closed as she realised how very wrong she had been about him. He was by no means as hard as nails—and he was not half as tough, or insensitive, as she'd assumed him to be.

'By then I was in university,' he said at length, 'and my father was living with an aunt who had been widowed, his sister. She took him under her roof solely to give me a break, to give me a chance to finish my education. I didn't see much of him in those days, not even in the holidays, simply because I couldn't stand it. I couldn't stand to see what he was doing to himself, how he was ruining himself, how he *had* ruined himself. Maybe I was intolerant at that age, I don't know, but I couldn't bear to witness waste of any description. In people, I mean, and some people could be forgiven for thinking me insensitive. I wasn't really, I just——'

'Don't.' Softly, Rebecca interrupted him. 'Stop there, please, I don't want to go on with this pretence.' Nor did she—she had taken his point and suddenly she was looking at the past very differently. She understood now. Him, and herself. Of course his intention had been to help her, even if it hadn't felt like that at the time.

And he had succeeded.

'I had an awful crush on you,' she said suddenly. 'Did you know that?'

'I suspected it.' He smiled, a smile that lit up his eyes and changed his features. 'No, that's not true. Of course I knew, I banked on it.'

'Banked on it?'

'I hoped that I would be able to get through to you where others failed—because you cared so much about what I thought of you.'

'Others didn't try very hard.' She shrugged, returning his smile. 'Others were content to let me be exactly who and what I was.'

'Don't knock that,' he cautioned her, his smile fading somewhat. 'That can be a very loving thing to do.'

'Yes,' she conceded. 'Yes, I see what you're saying. But when one is so young, one needs guidance, firmness, for one's own sake.'

'Right. It is different with children. I agree, they need guidelines.'

'And my parents did indulge me. And, you know,' she confessed, 'very, very often I secretly wished they would be firmer with me.' Then she was laughing. 'But when *you* were, I hated you for it!'

He was laughing, too. 'I noticed. Oh, I noticed that, Rebecca!'

A silence fell between them, a contented kind of silence which didn't need to be filled.

'Shall we go?' They had spoken simultaneously and, as if it were the most natural thing in the world, Becky's fingers slid around his the instant he held out his hand to her.

An hour later they were on their second cup of coffee. Lunch had not been the best she'd ever had but the view most certainly was. Halfway through their meal she had glanced out of the restaurant window—only to discover she couldn't see anything because of the cloud. It had been swirling thickly around the building. Now, it had gone again and the sky was an azure blue.

'There's one more thing you should see before we leave,' Stirling told her as they left the restaurant. 'Follow me.'

He led the way into a twisting cave carved out of solid ice. In it there were torch lights that gave it an eerie hue. Behind each of them was a rounded hollow where their heat had melted the ice and at some points she could almost see through it to the world outside. The place was damp and slippery—they were walking on wooden planks which Becky missed from time to time, her sneakers getting squelchy wet when she missed her footing. But it was worth it—it was fascinating. Delightedly she followed Stirling as the cave opened and narrowed—then she missed her footing completely and crashed into him.

'Rebecca! Are you all right?' He spun around and caught hold of her. With one hand on his shoulder and the other on the icy wet wall, she managed to catch her breath and to nod.

His other arm came swiftly around her and he pulled her closer, enabling her to get back on to the wooden planks. By then she was laughing and breathless. 'I'm OK, I've just got sodden feet and...' And she wasn't laughing any more. His eyes were boring into hers in the semi-darkness and suddenly she was acutely aware of his body next to hers. She could feel the warmth of it, the hardness of it, and for long seconds she couldn't breathe at all. He seemed so big as he looked down at her, making her feel petite by comparison, which she wasn't. He was so...so solid, and that in turn made her conscious of the softness of her breasts, pressed against him as he held her firmly.

And still he was looking into her eyes, his face only inches from hers, his breath making a faint mist in the chill air. She was convinced he was going to kiss her, and, with everything in her, to her own astonishment, she hoped very much that he would.

But he didn't kiss her. Instead he put her firmly, rather too firmly, away from him, as if kissing her was the very last thing he wanted to do in life.

CHAPTER FOUR

By ELEVEN o'clock the Bachmanns' anniversary party was in full swing and the villa was thronged with people of various nationalities. Some were dancing on the patio, on which coloured lights had been strung, some were standing in groups, chatting, and some seemed more interested in the buffet than in anything else. It was a magnificent spread. Caterers had been brought in and some of them were circulating now with trays of champagne. A bar had been set up in the dining-room, in addition to the one that was housed permanently in the living-room, and Becky looked around and thought of how many, many parties she had been to in the past few years.

Her eyes moved across the room to seek out Stirling. He hadn't asked her to dance, at least not yet, and it was bothering her. He had exchanged only a few words with her since the party got under way but it had, at the time, seemed like a good beginning.

'Stunning,' he'd said when she walked into the room. 'I thoroughly approve, Rebecca.'

He had been referring to her dress. She had chosen something fairly demure rather than the one she had planned to wear and was dressed in white satin, in a sleeveless but high-necked garment that was simplicity itself. Her hair was brushed loosely around her shoulders and she had made up only very lightly.

Stirling had smiled in unconcealed admiration, and she had thought then that the evening would prove to be as successful as their day had been . . . yet he seemed to be keeping his distance.

There had been no shortage of partners for her, of course; in fact there was one man who wouldn't leave her alone. He was Franz Schumacher, one of the Bachmanns' neighbours and an old friend of Ingrid's. He had, Ingrid had said when introducing Becky to him, been a friend of hers since childhood.

'When I was eight,' she had added laughingly, 'I asked Franz to marry me—and he said no. He was fifteen at the time. Five years later he married a German girl but it didn't last, so he divorced her and married an Italian.'

'And I divorced her,' Franz put in pointedly, 'about six months ago.'

'So play your cards right,' Ingrid had gone on mischievously, 'because if nothing else comes from this introduction, you'll at least be able to get all the jewellery you'd like at a generous discount. Franz owns one of the biggest jewellery shops in Lucerne—don't you, darling?'

Franz had loved that, Ingrid's flirting and joking. Like Stirling he was tall, blond and also good-looking. The difference was that he knew it and he played on it. Becky had taken a dislike to him but she couldn't seem to get rid of him. She had danced with him several times for two reasons only: firstly she could hardly refuse in the circumstances and secondly she wanted Stirling to see that she didn't have an aversion to dancing.

Neither did he. She had wondered about this, but no, he was dancing right now on the patio with Isabelle and he had already danced for a solid half-hour with Heidi. Clearly he loved to dance, so why wasn't he asking her?

She turned to Franz Schumacher. 'Franz, I really must sit down for a while. Would you be kind enough to bring

me something to eat, please? Pick anything you like,
I'm not fussy.'

'A pleasure!' He bowed and took himself off, looking
happy to be of service. Becky promptly detached herself
and found a seat in the corner of the living-room, by
the open, sliding doors.

Moments later Ingrid joined her. She did not look
pleased. 'What's with big, blond and beautiful?'

'You mean Franz? He's gone to——'

'I mean Stirling, as you know full well. Is he con-
fining himself to the over forties? There are lots of
younger women here—why hasn't he danced with any
of us?'

Becky shrugged. 'From what I've gathered, you have
a distinct disadvantage.'

'I have? What's that?'

'You're beautiful.'

'What? So what are you telling me? I'm beautiful but
I'm not his type? What man doesn't like a blue-eyed
blonde?'

'A rare one. But you're missing the point. Stirling is
unimpressed by beautiful women, that's one of the things
I learned about him today. He can take 'em or leave
'em.'

It was not what Becky had intended, but Ingrid took
that as a challenge. Her shoulders, naked in the
backless—and almost frontless—dress she had on,
squared suddenly. She stood, smoothing down the skirt
of the garment, and winked broadly at her girlfriend.
'We'll see about that! I'm going into action. What's that
saying you have about Mohammed and the mountain?
Watch this!'

And off she went. Surreptitiously Becky watched.
Ingrid's 'Excuse me' to her mother went as smoothly as

Ingrid herself did—right into Stirling's arms. But he held her at a distance and his smile was no more than polite.

Becky, finding herself faced with more food than she had wanted, glanced at them from time to time, trying hard not to laugh. Ingrid would not be pleased by her lack of progress; she wasn't used to that, and Stirling was still keeping her at a respectable distance.

'Becky?'

'Mm? I'm sorry, Franz, what did you say?'

'I said I've never seen eyes as green as yours. They're like emeralds.'

'So says the jeweller!'

'I'm serious. They're very beautiful.'

'I—thank you. I'm sorry if I sounded flippant.' She almost felt sorry for him then, he was trying so hard, making no attempt to hide how very attracted to her he was.

'Would you consider——' He was interrupted by the deep and unmistakable voice of Bruno Bachmann.

'Franz, what is this? You are monopolising my favourite guest and I shall have no more of it! Becky, how would you like to dance with an old man?'

She smiled, appearing to consider for a moment. 'Not very much, but I'd be delighted to dance with you, Bruno.' She handed her empty plate to Franz and got up, putting her hand into Bruno's as he led her outside. It was a perfect evening—the sky was studded with stars and the moon was almost full.

Bruno remarked on it as he took Becky into his arms. He was a good dancer and she enjoyed herself with him. She did catch Ingrid's eye, though, and she read in it the subtle but unmistakable message that Ingrid wanted a word in private. When it was appropriate to do so she detached herself from Bruno and went upstairs to her room.

Ingrid appeared a few minutes later. 'I'm getting precisely nowhere! What's with him? What happened with you two today? I was quite sick that I couldn't go out with you. Is it you he fancies?'

Becky laughed at that. 'I seriously doubt it. And nothing happened today except——'

'Except what?' Ingrid was looking at her suspiciously and Becky laughed again.

'Except that I realised how much I'd misjudged him. We talked a lot, got to know each other, we laughed a lot, too. I suppose you could say we made friends.'

'And that's it?'

'That's it, Ingrid. It and all there is to tell. But what I said to you earlier was true, he seems to have a thing about certain women—or maybe he doesn't like models. Yes, come to think of it he does seem to have a down on models. Or modelling. Or something.'

Ingrid was shaking her head. 'That's nonsense, utter nonsense.'

'Maybe, but it's accurate.'

Her friend would hear none of it, she wasn't going to give up. 'Is there anything else you can tell me about him? Any clues I could do with?'

'I don't think so.'

'Then I'll keep working on him. Come on, we'd better go back to the party, it's almost midnight and there are umpteen toasts lined up. Fancy being married to the same person for twenty-five years! It's not bad, is it? Is my hair OK?'

During the toasts, Franz Schumacher attached himself to Becky again and when all the speeches were over he asked her if she would like to go for a drive with him.

'Now? Do you mean now?'

'Why not? We could be forgiven for disappearing now. I thought you might like some fresh air——'

'You seem determined not to let Rebecca out of your sight, Franz.' The voice came from behind Becky and she turned quickly, feeling an undeniable pleasure at the hint of annoyance in it. Stirling's face was impassive but she was sure about that hint of annoyance. 'I was just about to ask Rebecca to dance with me,' he went on, turning to look at her. 'So I hope you're not about to depart?'

'No, I'm not. Well, Franz,' she said lightly, 'if you'll excuse me?'

His bow was stiffly polite. 'Of course.'

Stirling laughed as he led her to the patio. 'I thought you needed rescuing, Rebecca. You didn't seem to be enjoying yourself much.'

'Franz is pleasant enough,' she said non-committally. And what was she supposed to make of this? Was Stirling asking her to dance because he wanted to dance with her—or because he was merely being kind in 'rescuing' her?

The music changed as they reached the patio. It was slow and smoochy but Stirling began by holding her at the same respectable distance he had kept with his other partners.

'Rebecca? I said, a penny for your thoughts?' He laughed, pulling her fractionally closer as they moved in time to the music.

All she was aware of was his nearness, the faint whiff of his aftershave and the renewed shock of her body in contact with his. It evoked the memory of them standing in the ice cave in a contact much closer than this . . . and of the way she had wanted him to kiss her.

Sharply she pulled herself together, reminding herself that she was no longer the teenager who'd had a painful crush on this man—so what had got into her? Why was her mind running riot, and why did she have to be so acutely physically aware of him? 'I—wasn't thinking about anything in particular, I was just enjoying myself.'

'Quite right, too. At moments like this one shouldn't think at all, one should just enjoy.'

But she couldn't stop thinking. She was very attracted to Stirling regardless of—anything. How this had come about she would never know, but there it was. She turned her head fractionally to look at him, only to find that his eyes were intent upon her. There was an intensity in them she couldn't fathom, and then his sudden, 'Rebecca, there's something I should mention——'

'OK, you two, break it up! Coffee's being served in the dining-room.' It was Ingrid, laughing and flashing her fabulous smile at Stirling. 'And in any case it's my turn to dance with Stirling.'

'It'll be my pleasure,' he said, while inwardly Becky fumed at her friend's ill-timed interruption.

Ingrid did not get to dance with him again, though; the three of them joined the dwindling party indoors and sat making small talk. Within half an hour Ingrid was complaining of a headache and Becky knew from experience what that heralded. 'She's coming down with a cold,' she told Stirling, after Ingrid had reluctantly departed for bed. 'I know the signs. She gets them often. It's probably due to that drenching she got yesterday when we were shopping.'

'A pity,' Stirling said, but then he would. Becky had observed that his responses to Ingrid were no more than polite—but never less than polite.

She glanced around the room. Almost everyone had left. It was past two in the morning and the caterers had started to clear away.

Stirling broke the silence between them. 'What are your plans for tomorrow, Rebecca?'

'I haven't made any. I was hoping Ingrid and I could do something but, knowing her, she'll be spending the day in bed.'

There was, as there had been the previous night when the same suggestion had been made by someone else, just the slightest hesitation before he asked her to spend the day with him. 'If you have nothing better to do, of course,' he added. Then, laughingly, 'But madam, let's be quite clear on this: if you accept, you will make no sudden changes to our plans in the morning.'

'Proposed changes,' she pointed out, having every intention of accepting. 'I only proposed changes this morning—and where did it get me?'

'Ten thousand feet up a mountain.'

'Exactly! So what good would it do me to argue with you?'

'None at all.' Their eyes met and she laughed, but inwardly she knew a vague sense of discomfort. It was difficult to pinpoint but she had the oddest feeling that Stirling had asked her out almost against his will. There had been that repeated hesitation. And tonight he had kept his distance for hours, until he'd rescued her from Franz. Why?

'Let's hope that Ingrid's feeling all right,' she went on, 'so she can come with us.'

Ingrid was not feeling all right. When Becky went to her room at nine the following morning, she found her friend in a fit of sneezing and snuffling. 'You've got another cold, Ingrid.'

'You don't say! Stop looking so cheerful, will you? What do you want?'

'I came to see if you were fit to come out with——'

'No way.'

'With me and Stirling.'

'I see!' With a hearty blow of her nose, Ingrid pulled herself into a sitting position, looking disgusted. 'You must have moved quickly with him after I went to bed last night. Incapacitated,' she added dramatically.

'Look, I'm only going out with him because——'

'Because you fancy him. And don't argue. It's me you're talking to, remember. Apart from which, he fancies you.'

'No, you're quite wrong about that, Ingrid. He's only being——'

'He fancies you. Which is fine with me,' she added, shrugging. 'I must be getting dense in my old age. Last night I thought I was in with a chance, but no. I gave it my best try and I made it quite clear how the land lay, but no. He couldn't take his eyes off you.'

'That's a wild exaggeration——'

Ingrid ignored that. 'For the record, I am green with envy. But good luck to you,' she went on, grinning. 'I'll look forward to seeing you later and hearing how you got on.'

The conversation bothered Rebecca, though she didn't know why. 'Listen, do you think it's rude of us to go out when——?'

'Don't be silly. There's no way my mother and father will feel up to much, after last night's party, and in any case their friends are here for a few days. So go—go and enjoy!'

Becky retreated from the sick-room wishing Ingrid well. 'If you're not fit to come downstairs, I'll have dinner in here with you tonight, to cheer you up.'

'No, you won't,' came the firm reply. 'You'll be going out to dinner with Stirling, just wait and see. He's keen, I tell you.'

Rebecca made no further comment, but she could not deny that she was glad she would have Stirling to herself. She wanted to know more about him.

'I'd like you to tell me more about yourself.' They were in the Rolls, driving into Lucerne in order to pick up the steamer. Stirling had suggested they sail across the lake, and that they have lunch in what he described as an idyllic spot which he was sure she would like.

'It's funny you should say that.' She turned to look at him as he drove. He was wearing pale blue trousers and a darker blue shirt which was open at the neck. He looked cool and crisp and very much in control as he eased the big motor car down the winding road into the town. 'Because I was going to say the same thing to you.'

'You first.' He glanced at her, smiling, his eyes moving swiftly and appreciatively over her. The white shorts and shirt she had on made a perfect foil for her ever deep-ening suntan and she knew she looked good. Her hair was in a French plait, her skin free of make-up.

'Well, I've already brought you up to date as far as my family's concerned—and I don't think there's much else I can add about myself. Modelling is hard work, whether you believe it or not——'

'Actually, I do,' he interrupted. 'But I wasn't thinking along those lines, I was wondering what you have planned for your future, if anything.'

'Oh, I have plans all right. I intend to go into business when I'm over the hill.'

'Over the hill?'

'Modelling is a very competitive business, as I'm sure you also know, and when I've had my day I'm going to open a boutique. It'll be something rather special, up-market and stocked with clothes with a difference.'

'I take it that you'll do the buying?'

'Of course.'

'Have you any experience of that?'

'Of buying, no, but I know where to go to find what I want. I know quite a lot about the theory, too, if I can put it that way.'

'So you don't see yourself settling down?'

Rebecca laughed at that. 'Compared to the life I lead now, that *will* be settled down!'

'But you're not discontented with your life currently, are you?'

'Not at all.'

'And where will your business be? In London?'

'About that I have no idea, not at this stage.' She turned to him again, noticing suddenly that he had two freckles on the top of his ear. She smiled inwardly. Oh, how she had hated her own scattering of freckles when she was younger! She had put lemon juice on them in an effort to get rid of them—an old wives' remedy that definitely didn't work.

'Rebecca? Have I lost you?'

'No. Sorry, I was just thinking about the past.' When he shot her a deliberately wary look, she laughed aloud. 'No, no, not about you and your nagging. I was wondering about your father. Did he die during your last year at university?'

'During the last term. He was still living with my aunt, in the Lake District, and as far as I was concerned that was home because our own house had been sold long

since. And all the money had gone. So home I went to
the Lake District and—well, I had a rest and stayed on
with my aunt for a couple of months. Then I moved to
London and I didn't keep in touch with anyone except
my aunt. I was admittedly... disquietened, if that's the
right word.'

Upset, was what he meant. Naturally. His own years
as a teenager had been bad ones. But, unlike her, he had
been unable to do anything about that, he'd been unable
to change his circumstances.

'Here we are. A stroke of luck, Rebecca.' They were
sliding into a parking slot very close to the place where
the steamer awaited. Once they were on it, Stirling got
two cups of coffee and they sat on the upper deck,
sipping it and admiring the view around them.

'And it gets better.' Stirling touched her shoulder
lightly as he pointed across the lake to the Casino and
to various other buildings. Then the boat moved off and
as far as Becky was concerned, the next few hours were
a glimpse of Paradise. The day was perfect, windless but
for the light breeze created by the steamer's motion.
There was so much colour around: the clear blue of the
sky and the deeper blue of the lake, the mountains and
the trees making a perfect back-drop.

Becky was wide-eyed, drinking it all in with pleasure.
'It's certainly the stuff that——' She had been going to
say something about picture-postcards but she forgot the
rest of the sentence because again she had turned to find
Stirling regarding her intently. This time, however, the
intensity in the grey eyes was of a different nature; he
seemed to be looking at her with a new regard, a
new... respect... as if she had done or said something
that had pleased him enormously. But she had done
nothing. 'What is it?' There was puzzlement in her voice.

'Nothing.' He glanced away. 'I—was just enjoying your enjoyment.'

They had lunch in a small, open-air café on the edge of the lake. The steamer had pulled away with several children on board waving to the few people who got off, including Becky and Stirling. So in effect they were stranded until the next boat came along—but what a spot to be stranded in! There were flowers everywhere, in tubs surrounding them, on bushes, on trellises along the walls and in vases on the red and white checked tablecloths.

'So what do you think of *sauerkraut*? You say you've never had it before?'

'I think—well, it's not bad, but I don't think I'll be ordering it again.' Becky looked up at her companion dubiously, pulling a face which was meant to convey her opinion more graphically. *Sauerkraut* was ... so-so. The *rosti* potatoes and the beef which went with it, on the other hand, were going down very well. 'Anyway, bring me up to date. After leaving university and then the Lake District, you set off for London determined to make your fortune?'

Stirling nodded, refilling her wine glass and answering her as if it had been a serious question. 'Too right. And I've been very lucky.'

'Rubbish. I'm told you're a genius when it comes to handling money.'

'When it comes to handling money ...' He broke off, musing, giving Becky the impression that he was finishing the sentence in his head. He was, which left her wondering what thoughts had been triggered.

'I've done all right, Rebecca. No, that's not true. I'm a millionaire several times over,' he said. But he said it with a shrug, without any conceit or even pride. Somehow, he seemed not to care.

'Come on, Stirling, you're not going to tell me that it's made you unhappy?'

He looked up quickly, his eyes narrowing thoughtfully as they gazed steadily into hers. 'No, I'm not. But it hasn't made me happy, either.'

'Well, they say that happiness is something money can't buy.'

'And they,' he said, smiling at last, 'are right, whoever they are. Now, what would you say to some ice-cream?'

She giggled, unable to resist, feeling inexplicably light-hearted. 'Hello, ice-cream.'

'Aha! Perhaps I've been wrong about you, Rebecca Hill. I think there might be just a tiny trace of humour in you, after all.'

'And perhaps I've been wrong about you,' she countered, her green eyes dancing with pleasure. 'I think you're not *quite* the brute I'd been convinced you were.'

It was during the afternoon, when they were sailing across the lake back to Lucerne, that things changed between them, when Stirling remarked on Becky's enjoyment of the simple things. 'You're enjoying this just as much as you did the first time, aren't you? The simple things seem to please you.'

She was leaning against the rail of the steamer as it cut its path through the crystal water, eyes down, smiling, feeling happy and content. All day she had been enjoying herself, enjoying a sense of freedom, all kinds of freedom—most especially the freedom of not caring what time it was or even what day it was. 'It's this place, all of it. It has a certain magic, it has everything, it's just so beautiful and——'

And what? Whatever else she had been going to add, she promptly forgot because this time when she turned to face Stirling she saw on his face an expression of unmistakable tenderness. He was leaning on the rail about two feet away from her, watching her, his smile so attractive that her breath caught in her throat. Very quietly, softly, he said, 'And so are you, Rebecca. Very beautiful...'

For seconds she couldn't speak. She wanted to be flippant, to tease him with her answer, remind him of the irrelevance, but it didn't work out like that. To her surprise she found her own voice was soft when finally it came. 'Thank you, Stirling.'

It was happening again—she was wishing him closer, wishing herself in his arms, hoping he would kiss her. There was no danger of that, though; for one thing there were dozens of other people on board the steamer and for another, he obviously didn't want to.

She was wrong. This time he did kiss her, albeit very briefly to begin with. He caught hold of her chin and let his lips brush lightly over hers, as if it were more than he could do to resist. There was no resistance at all in Becky. Of their own volition her arms lifted to encircle his neck and in the instant they did so his arms came tightly around her back. He pulled her into him and kissed her in earnest, the pressure of his mouth easing her lips apart so he could taste of her more deeply.

It wasn't until later that she thought about her reaction, about the immediate sense of intoxication she experienced. She returned his kiss gently, revelling in the strength of his arms around her, moving fractionally so the entire length of her body was in contact with his.

It was the loud, raucous cheer from somewhere behind them that broke the spell. They pulled apart and turned to see several teenagers laughing, making gestures of encouragement. They were German, by the sound of it, and Becky thought it just as well that she couldn't understand a word they were saying.

Stirling smiled at them with good humour, but he glanced down at Becky with a look of apology. 'Sorry about that.'

Of course she thought he was apologising about the youngsters—until he moved away from her, well away. At that point she became unsure. A frown creased her brow. He seemed displeased with himself.

When next he spoke his voice was hard. 'You accept compliments very graciously. I find that surprising. You must have been told a million times how beautiful you are.'

What could she say to that? 'I—have been told.' In an attempt to regain their earlier mood she added laughingly, 'But not that often!'

It didn't work, it didn't even provoke a smile. Again she frowned, reaching out a hand to touch his shoulder. 'Stirling, please tell me...I'm aware that you think beauty is only skin deep, and I agree with you, but...have you been hurt by someone beautiful?'

'Yes and no,' he said, before pointing out something in the distance and effectively changing the subject.

She said nothing further. She let silence stand between them until he broke it. 'Rebecca, I ought to...' He stopped there. He had looked at her then turned away, his eyes fixed on the water.

'Go on,' she said.

'I was just wondering if we could do this again tomorrow.'

'Of course.' Her answer came without thought; she didn't need to think about it. She was distracted in any case because he had not been about to say that, welcome though it was. He'd been about to say something else but he'd changed his mind, she just knew it. She shrugged inwardly, realising it couldn't have been important. 'I'll look forward to it,' she added, pleased to see him smiling again.

CHAPTER FIVE

'You look like the cat that got the cream. Tell me everything, Becky.'

'There's nothing to tell, really.' Rebecca smiled at her friend sympathetically. Ingrid looked quite unwell.

'Don't give me that! If there's nothing to tell, why are you grinning like an idiot?'

'Am I?' Was she? She hoped not—but she was certainly feeling happy. She smiled again. 'I'll admit that I've had a wonderful, wonderful day. Stirling is a delightful companion.'

'A delightful companion.' Ingrid looked disgusted. 'What tripe. Don't be flowery with me, Becky Hill. Get to the point instead.'

'There isn't a point.' Rebecca sat at the foot of Ingrid's bed, knowing, now, that she was grinning like an idiot. She couldn't seem to help it.

'For God's sake...you're not falling for him, are you?'

'Don't be ridiculous, Ingrid. I like him a lot—but that's all.'

There was a frown, a long and searching look. 'Well, I don't know. I'm not sure. There's something different about you. Your eyes are too bright or something. Is he taking you out to dinner tonight?'

'No. He wanted to but——'

'I told you!' There was triumph in Ingrid's voice. 'Don't tell me you refused because of me?'

'Of course I did. I knew how much you'd be missing me.'

Again there was a look of disgust. 'Oh, yes? As if I don't see enough of you as it is.'

'Thanks.'

'Seriously, though, why the devil didn't you accept the date tonight?'

'Because I'm spending the day with him again tomorrow.'

'Ahh. Right. That makes more sense——'

'And I *do* want to spend some time with you.'

'Then where are you going now?'

'To shower and change, then I'll be right back and we'll have dinner in here together. I'm hot and sticky...'

'If you ask me, you're hot and bothered...' Ingrid put in as Rebecca closed the bedroom door behind her.

She got to her own room with those words echoing round her head. Hot and bothered. It was then that she thought about her response when Stirling had kissed her. How immediate her reaction, and how strong! But why was she surprised? She had already admitted to herself how much she was attracted to him; the pull was there constantly, and it wasn't only one way, either. He was every bit as attracted to her, she was certain of that. What she didn't understand was the way he seemed to hold back from her, in more ways than one. She still had the feeling that he'd kissed her against his will— which made no sense at all. Unless...maybe she reminded him of someone? The one who had hurt him? And what had he meant, when he'd answered her question about that. Yes and no, he'd said. What should she make of that?

Feeling vaguely annoyed with herself, she shook her head and looked at her reflection in the bathroom mirror, saying aloud, 'What's the matter with you, Rebecca? Why are you fretting about that?' It was a good question and she leaned forward, inspecting her face carefully.

She had definitely had enough sun today; a good coating of moisturiser was in order. As for her eyes...Ingrid was right...there was an added light in them.

'How come you're not at the office today?'

It was ten o'clock on the Monday morning and Rebecca and Stirling were sitting close together on the funicular railway. It was chugging its way slowly up what he had described as a 'little' mountain, the 'prettiest' in the area. 'It is Monday today, isn't it? You have offices in Berne as well as Zurich, don't you?'

'Yes, and yes again.' Stirling looked at her, smiling. 'And to answer your first question—I don't feel like going to work.'

She laughed at that, looking about her at the magnificent scenery, all of which was drenched in sunshine. They were being very fortunate with the weather. 'Can't say I blame you in this weather.'

He laughed, too, seeming delighted for some reason. 'Ah, Rebecca, how sweet you are at times! The weather has nothing to do with it, I simply don't feel like working just now. Remember that I pay lots of other people to do that.'

'Does this happen often?' she asked, deliberately making it sound like an illness.

'When I allow it to. You see, your old friend,' he added, his grey eyes twinkling, 'has learnt many things since you saw him ten years ago.'

'You mean you've turned into a hedonist?'

'A hedonist? Perhaps. I meant that I've learned to be gentle with myself. And why not? If something makes you happy, why not do it?'

She would have taken him seriously had it not been for the flash of pain she saw in his eyes. It was gone as rapidly as it had appeared but it had been unmistakable.

Worse, it affected her in a way that shocked her; her heart started beating abnormally quickly and once again she had an overwhelming desire to hold him and be held by him. 'Sounds like a dangerous condition to me,' she said, feeling the need to say something.

'Not at all. Isn't this what you're doing, too?'

'I'm resting.'

'There's no need to defend yourself. At your age, how many days' rest do you need before you're recovered?'

'At my age? Now listen, Grandad——'

'You're evading the point.'

So she was. And she was laughing.

'Rebecca, why don't you just say you don't feel like going back to work yet?'

'OK, I don't feel like going back to work yet!'

'That's better. You can afford time off so you're having time off.' He moved closer to her, his blond hair glinting beautifully as a shaft of sunlight caught it. 'I'm glad I got that out of you,' he said, suddenly serious. 'Glad to hear you're not talking in terms of "should" or "ought" or "duty". There are too many of those in life—and do you know something? They are invariably imposed by ourselves.'

'I—yes, I suppose you're right.' She frowned, considering. 'I have to say it's nice, pleasing myself as I am at the moment.'

'Then why do I hear a hint of guilt?' he probed, startling her with his accuracy.

'Because really I ought—I mean I should make a duty visit—I mean——' She broke off, laughing wholeheartedly. When she calmed down again, at his prompting she explained herself. 'My parents are missing me and I said I'd see them for a few days before I start work again.'

'But you don't want to go?'

'It isn't that,' she said honestly. 'It's just—well, I'm enjoying myself so much here, I want to stay on for a while.'

'Then stop feeling guilty, allow yourself to do just that.' He caught hold of her hand and held it in his own.

He still had hold of her hand when they disembarked and started walking, letting go of it only when he stopped to take some photographs of her.

'I should have had this with me yesterday.' He indicated the camera. 'It's rotten luck that your legs are hidden from me today.'

Becky had put on a pale pink cotton dress. She was also wearing a wide-brimmed hat in order to keep the sun off her face. Stirling had been delighted by it—hence the camera.

'To work,' he said. 'I want you to go and stand by that lovely old relic of a wall and do whatever you would do in front of a professional photographer.'

Becky did just that. But she started by making faces and laughed like a drain when Stirling protested that she was wasting his film.

Their entire day was like that, full of laughter and jokes, with occasional snatches of serious conversation. They talked about anything and everything and there was no more holding back. Stirling caught hold of her often, his arm going around her waist or her shoulders. He didn't kiss her again, but then there was hardly a moment when they weren't around other people—until they got back to his car.

'Rebecca, I want to thank you.' He turned to her, his voice serious to the point of intensity.

'For what?' She was a little startled, she couldn't begin to interpret the look in the grey eyes fixed so firmly on hers.

'For your company, for the day. I love talking to you. Believe me, I haven't enjoyed myself so much in...' He broke off, shaking his head. In one sudden and swift movement she was in his arms, his mouth was on hers and he was kissing her far more forcefully than he had previously. Becky stiffened slightly, knowing that his intention was to convey something he wouldn't or couldn't say to her. But alongside that there was something about the force of his kiss that spelled anger. It was not at her, she knew, but it was there nevertheless.

'Stirling.' She pulled away, her eyes searching his. 'What is it? What's wrong?'

For all the world, it was just as if she had slapped him. For a second he stared at her. Then he blinked, shaking his head again. 'Yes, you're right. I'm sorry. Perhaps that was a mistake...'

She put her hand on his as his fingers closed too tightly around the steering wheel. She had seen the white of his knuckles. 'It wasn't a mistake as far as I'm concerned,' she said gently. 'But I have the unwelcome feeling you were thinking of someone else just now.'

'I was,' he said baldly. 'And I can only apologise for that.'

When they got back to the villa, Isabelle greeted Becky with the news that Franz Schumacher had telephoned. 'He was wondering if you'd have dinner with him tonight.'

'I wondered how long it would take him to call,' Stirling put in, a comment Becky pretended not to hear.

'I'll—ring him back.' She excused herself to do just that, from Ingrid's room.

'Hi!' Ingrid was reading a magazine, looking thoroughly bored. 'I'm feeling rotten, before you ask. Now sit down and tell me everything—and don't say there's nothing to tell.'

'There's nothing to tell.'

Ingrid's eyes narrowed. She subjected her friend to another searching look before making her pronouncement. 'Oh, yes, there is. And you, my darling, are in trouble. You're falling for that man. You are also in for a shock.'

Ingrid wasn't smiling, either—she meant what she'd said. 'You'd better sit down, Becky—I kid you not.'

Rebecca sat, feeling a sudden, inexplicable shaft of fear cut through her. She looked at Ingrid with fear, too, though she didn't realise it.

Ingrid plunged straight in. 'I was quizzing my father about Stirling today, very casually of course, and guess what? You were right about his attitude to models and modelling—or both. Stirling is married to a model.'

CHAPTER SIX

'OR RATHER,' Ingrid added as if it mattered, 'an ex-model.'

'Married?' Becky tried and failed to dissemble. The news came as a shock, there was no hiding it. What worried her was her sense of disappointment, it was enormous. 'He's—Ingrid, are you sure?'

'Sure I'm sure.' And she, unlike Becky, was not at all put out, or put off, by this piece of information. 'My father's only known Stirling personally for about two years and there wasn't much he could tell me, but he did say that he had married a model about three years ago. There's no mistake. It was when Daddy first showed him a photograph of me; apparently Stirling said I looked a lot like his wife.'

'Could it have been ex-wife, perhaps?'

'His *wife*. That's what my father said he said. Stirling said she was an ex-model but he did not say ex-wife. There was no "ex" in it.'

'So where is she?'

'How the devil do I know? And so what? Daddy's never met the woman so one thing is obvious, it's not a healthy marriage. And if I'm his wife's look-alike, no wonder I couldn't get anywhere with Stirling! I mean, according to Daddy she's never come to Switzerland with him.'

'Not to Bruno's knowledge.'

'No, she never has. My parents have been to Stirling's house here often. There was never a wife there. Becky?

What is it? You've gone pale. For heaven's sake, I know he's gorgeous but—oh, lord, you *have* fallen for him, haven't you?'

'Oh, Ingrid, don't be ridiculous! I'm just—taken aback, that's all.'

'You mean you're shocked rigid.'

'Yes. OK. I'm shocked rigid.'

'Well, don't say anything to him, will you? I mean——'

'I know what you mean. But I can't guarantee that, Ingrid. I'm angry and I'm...hurt,' she admitted. 'I'll *try* not to say anything.' But why hadn't he said something? Why hadn't he mentioned this when he'd told her about his life? How could he have done that and omitted to mention something as major as a marriage? She felt sick inside—and she was fuming. She wanted to fly downstairs and confront Stirling, demand to be told why he had let her believe he was free. Of course she couldn't, she could only give vent to her feelings to Ingrid.

'Not a word,' she said harshly. 'Ingrid, he's never said a damn thing about this!'

'What's all the fuss?' That was typical of Ingrid—she had been out with lots of married men, had thought nothing of it, but that was not Becky's style.

'The fuss? I'll tell you what the fuss is, I hate deceit! It's unkind, unnecessary and I hate it. You know that.'

'I know it's your policy never to go out with married men—— '

'Too bloody right!' Becky shot to her feet. 'But I've got nothing against divorced ones.'

'Becky?' Ingrid was staring at her, at a loss to understand. 'What does that mean?'

'It means I'm going to accept Franz Schumacher's invitation to have dinner with him tonight.'

'Didn't Stirling ask you out?'

'No, as a matter of fact, he didn't. And even if he had,' she went on heatedly, 'I wouldn't be going—not after *this*.' She had to get out of the villa; she did not want to be in Stirling's company at all until she'd got over her anger. If she stayed in it would be too difficult to hide it—which would make Isabelle and Bruno feel awkward. 'What's Franz's number? I'll ring him back straight away——'

There was laughter at that. 'I shouldn't bother. Believe me, he might be the boy next door as far as I'm concerned but he's actually a womaniser first-class. Not your type at all. You'd be out of your depth with the likes of Franz.'

'Come off it! I've had experience with that type.'

'You, my friend, have had no experience at all.'

'Don't be silly, Ingrid, I've been taking care of myself for years, haven't I?'

Ingrid nodded dubiously, as if she weren't too sure about that. 'I suppose so, it depends on your point of view.' She gave Becky the number of Franz's home and watched with a cynical smile as her friend made her telephone call.

'Good grief!' She laughed uproariously as soon as Becky put the phone down. 'You came on a bit husky, didn't you? Well, don't say I didn't warn you!'

'Relax, Ingrid. You heard me ask him to take me somewhere typically touristy—I did that for a reason. He can't possibly have misunderstood me—it isn't going to be a quiet, romantic dinner.'

'Where did he suggest?'

'The Stadtkeller—if that's how you pronounce it.'

'Ha! Then no, it is *not* going to be a quiet, romantic dinner! You'll be lucky if you can hear yourselves think in there.'

Which suited Becky down to the ground. All she wanted was some distraction. She left the room hastily in order to have a word with Isabelle, knowing that Ingrid understood how she was feeling. She might not agree with Becky's reaction to the news of Stirling being married but she understood her well enough.

Isabelle was on the terrace, enjoying the last of the sinking sun with Stirling and Heidi. Bruno and Benedikt were nowhere to be seen. Becky glanced at the back of Stirling's blond head as she approached, forcing herself to be casual and calm before she looked at him.

It was he who spoke first, turning quickly in his chair as if he had sensed her presence. 'Ah, Rebecca! I was just telling the ladies about our day. I was saying that tomorrow I'm going to take you to Engelberg for lunch, then we'll drive further afield. I think you'll enjoy that. How does it sound?'

She was momentarily stuck for words. How did she answer? How, in the face of his enthusiasm, in the face of Isabelle's smiles, Heidi's interest? She thought of something. 'I'm—actually, I've been feeling guilty about leaving Ingrid alone. It doesn't seem fair——'

Everyone spoke at once. Isabelle looked horrified, and Heidi was saying something about opportunities not to be missed, while Stirling was reminding her about giving herself permission to enjoy herself without guilt. It was hopeless, no one was going to let her stay indoors on her holiday just because Ingrid had a cold. In that case, she would have to deal with tomorrow when it came...

Deliberately she glanced at her watch, keeping her tone light. 'Isabelle, I just came to tell you I won't be here for dinner tonight.'

There was a brief, puzzled silence. Given that Isabelle herself had passed on Franz's message, she seemed totally at a loss now. 'You won't?'

'No, I'm going out with Franz. Remember?'

'Oh! I wasn't at all sure you would accept, Becky.'

'Why ever not?' she said, laughing a little.

Stirling answered that one. 'Because he's twice divorced and his reputation as a lady-killer spreads way beyond Lucerne. Right, Isabelle?' He wasn't smiling; he seemed extremely put out, a reaction that left Becky barely able to contain an angry retort. How could he speak of Franz like this? What room had he to talk? He wasn't even divorced, he was *married*.

'Oh, I think Becky can look after herself,' Isabelle said, smiling at last. 'After all, she and my Ingrid have been—how do you say it?—defending their honour for several years now. At least, I hope they have!' she added, laughing in a way that made Becky wonder. Did she believe that, really?

A fleeting glance at Stirling told nothing of his reaction to that. It was Heidi alone who commented, amused by her old friend. 'Come now, Isabelle, did you, at their age?' With a sweep of her arm she gestured towards Becky. 'And you were never that beautiful!'

'I must go,' Becky said hastily, not caring for the turn in the conversation. She had no idea how much Ingrid's parents knew of her private life in London but one thing was for sure, it was very different from Becky's. 'I have to bathe and dress, if you'll excuse me...'

When Franz came to collect her that evening, Stirling was not around. Rebecca was glad of that, and she was glad too of Ingrid's warning because the moment she got into his car, she realised that her friend had been accurate. Franz turned to her smoothly, smiling his approval as his eyes took in every inch of her. She was quite casually clothed in a knitted dress in bottle-green but he was looking her over as if she were some kind of siren.

'You look good enough to eat, Becky, and speaking of that, let us not bother with the Stadtkeller. I know a quiet place which I think will be far more——'

'No.' The word came firmly but graciously. 'I particularly want to go where the tourists go. Surely you can understand that? You said there was a floor show, I'd like very much to see it.'

'Very well,' he shrugged, putting his low-slung sports car into gear. 'My wish is only to please you, beautiful lady.'

The Stadtkeller was a riot. It was a large restaurant, well lit and noisy with the sounds of laughter, voices, the clinking of glasses and the music from the show, which was already under way. Franz had to raise his voice in order to be heard across the table that separated them but Becky had not the slightest twinge of conscience about bringing him here. Hadn't he said he wanted to please her? Well, she was pleased—yet she was still raging inwardly. There was so much going on but it did nothing to quell her anger with Stirling.

As the evening continued she kept her chat to a minimum, concentrating instead on eating food she had never tasted before—and was hardly tasting now—and watching the entertainment. There was a display of flag-throwing, of alphorn playing—at which some of the audience were invited to try their hand—or rather their lungs—and a troupe who sang and danced and yodelled.

The wine helped to calm her, and Franz was not sparing with it. He kept refilling her glass and she let him, knowing what she was capable of drinking without losing her head. What she did lose was some of her anger, although she had no idea this would prove to be a temporary loss. Thoughts of Stirling got milder and milder as the hours passed—until she found herself able to look at the situation from a different perspective.

Why, she supposed, should he have told her about his private life? She had told him very little about her own—so why should she have expected it of him?

Because as far as yours is concerned, very little is all there is to tell.

Determinedly, she tried to ignore that voice in her head but it persisted. Had you been married, you wouldn't have neglected to mention the fact.

'Becky? I was just saying, it's very hot in here. If you're ready, we could go on to somewhere else...'

Franz had paid the bill some time ago. They had lingered and lingered but she could put off their departure no longer. She suggested they go for a walk, he suggested a drink elsewhere. 'You don't want to go on somewhere, Becky? But the night is so young! I thought perhaps a nightclub, the casino maybe or...'

He was right, the night was young, too young for her to go back to the villa. She simply didn't want to, not yet; she wanted to be met by no one, by nothing except silence when she got back to the villa.

But Franz was clearly not enamoured with the idea of a walk and when they got outside the matter was settled for them. It was raining. 'A pity,' Becky said. 'I could use some fresh air.'

'I have a covered terrace at my house,' Franz told her. 'We could sit out there and have a drink.' The words came casually enough but Becky laughed inwardly. There was no chance of that!

'No, thank you. I'll settle for a drive with the car window open.'

'Then we might as well drive to my place.' He slipped an arm around her waist as they walked hurriedly to his car. Becky removed it promptly but gently; Franz had been pleasant enough but he did nothing for her and there was no way she was going to encourage him to make a pass at her.

'Not your place, Franz. Just drive for a while— anywhere.'

He said nothing for a moment, until he was opening the passenger door for her, his eyes trailing appreciatively down the long length of her legs as she sat and swung them in. Then, with a smile he said, 'If that will make you happy, that is what we will do.'

'That's all I want,' she said, meaning it. She snuggled down into the bucket seat of his sports car, opened her window a little and closed her eyes.

Married. To an ex-model. And not a word about it!

She tried to tell herself she was silly to feel so hurt— but that didn't help. Her curiosity was just as strong, too. From what she had gathered, from what Ingrid had gathered, Stirling was estranged from his wife. So where was she? Why wasn't she here with him now?

She and Franz drove in silence and Becky appreciated that, the way he just left her alone and concentrated on his driving. Unfortunately it couldn't last.

'Becky? Why are you so quiet...?'

'I'm sorry, Franz, I'm getting rather tired. Perhaps we should head back to Lucerne now.' She glanced at the clock on the dashboard and decided enough was enough, they had been driving for quite a while and by the time they got back to the villa, everyone would surely be in bed. It was almost one o'clock now.

Franz laughed softly, slowing the car to a halt. There was no other vehicle on the road and, as far as Becky could see, they were in the middle of nowhere. When he made no attempt to turn around but cut the engine instead, she groaned inwardly. She should have known better than to do this. The man was a wolf and there was going to be a scene. Fortunately she knew her lines by heart and she knew how to deliver them.

Firmly, before he could even make a move, she said, 'Don't. Please, Franz. Let's just keep this on a friendly footing so no one will get offended. Just take me home.'

'Oh, nobody's going to be offended, beautiful lady. All I want to do is kiss you . . .'

'That's what they all say. Now please, I'm not playing games and I'm not——'

'That's what they all say.' He was laughing, countering her remark pleasantly.

So it was into phase two. Becky knew how to emasculate when necessary—but she didn't enjoy it. 'Franz, believe it or not, you are not my type.'

'Then why should you accept this date?' He reached for her, draping an arm around her shoulder. 'Suppose we find out?'

Very slowly, deliberately and coldly, she said, 'Let go of me.'

To her surprise he did—and it was more than she dared do to laugh, that would be unkind. It hadn't been difficult at all, she had plenty more lines in stock but she didn't need to use them. So much for the womaniser—he was firing the engine, obviously put-out, saying something about cold-blooded English girls and their attitudes to sex.

The silence during the drive back to the villa was inevitable. The atmosphere was strained and for his sake alone Becky tried to change it. She talked generalities but, when she got no more than a grunt in answer, she gave up. She really couldn't be bothered.

When he dropped her at the back of the villa, which was in darkness except for a single outside light, she thanked him and bade him goodnight. Franz did respond, he helped her out of the car and saw her safely to the door.

'Goodnight, Becky. I'll be in touch,' he added, which, if experience was anything to go by, was not to be taken seriously.

Gratefully she let herself in the back door with the key Isabelle had given her. All she wanted was a long drink of water and her bed. She flicked the kitchen light on and was standing at the sink when she heard someone else letting themselves in.

She spun round with a mixture of puzzlement and anxiety. The villa was pretty remote but—had she neglected to close the door properly?

In one way, she needn't have worried. It was Stirling, dressed in dark trousers and shirt and a leather jacket, his hair soaked with rain. 'Good grief, you startled me!'

'You startled me,' he said, walking into the room, shrugging out of his jacket. 'You've just got in, I take it?'

His tone brought every ounce of her anger right back to the surface. She glared at his broad-shouldered back as he draped his jacket over the back of a chair, wondering if she was mistaken in thinking he had sounded censorious. 'Yes, I have. And you? Do you often go walking in the rain?'

'Often.'

'At this hour?'

'At this hour.' He turned to face her, leaning against the wall, his voice and his manner unmistakable now. 'So what was all that about?'

'What?' Becky couldn't believe it. Surely he wasn't referring to her date with Franz?

He was—his eyes were examining her from head to foot, and what he said next was more than enough to increase her anger—and then some! 'You and Franz Schumacher, Rebecca. I'm referring to you and your dinner date and why you accepted it. If the look on your face is anything to go by, you didn't have much fun.'

'Now, just a minute——'

'In fact, it *looks* as if he didn't even get to first base with you,' he went on, ignoring her. 'You haven't got a hair out of place and your lipstick's perfect. Tell me, what——'

'For pity's sake!' she exploded. Her hands were shaking so hard that she almost dropped the glass she was holding. 'What is this—an interrogation? Mind your own business, Stirling, this has nothing to do with you!'

It didn't ruffle him, at least not outwardly. He continued to survey her as if for tell-tale signs and there was something incredibly hard about those slate-grey eyes, a look she had never seen before. 'I think it has.'

She realised, then, that what she could see in his eyes was anger. She was further incensed by that; why the hell should *he* be angry? 'Oh, really?' It was not what she wanted to say, the temptation to come out with what she knew was almost overwhelming, but the last thing she wanted to do in this house was to cause ill-feeling. 'Perhaps you'll explain that?'

'Certainly. I thought you were different, Rebecca.'

'Different from what?'

'From the impression you gave me that time in Heathrow Airport, one of a good-time girl. I had begun to feel sure, to think——'

'I don't care what you think, or thought, nor do I care for this conversation.' Good-time girl? What a nerve!

Very quietly he said, 'All I'm asking is how the land lies with you and Schumacher. You were warned about him but you went ahead regardless and I'd like to know what happened between your leaving the Stadtkeller and your getting back here.'

So he had been talking to Ingrid—not that that mattered, there was no way Becky was going to start explaining herself! She put the glass on the draining board and walked away from him without another word.

She nearly got as far as the door.

'No, you don't!' He spoke as he caught hold of her roughly, spinning her round to face him. 'You don't walk away from me this time.'

'Let go of me, Stirling! How dare you?'

'Answer my question and you're free.'

There it was again, the perfect invitation for a retort that would tell him she knew he was not free. Again she resisted, glaring at him instead, undaunted by the size of him, the way he dwarfed her own considerable height. Somehow she managed to answer without shouting, probably because she was aware that her hosts' bedroom was on this level of the villa. 'I'm perfectly capable of fending off the Franz Schumachers of this world . . . *if I wish to.*'

Something seemed to snap inside him. His eyes blazed into hers with a passion she could not understand. 'Damn it, if you won't answer my question then I'll have to learn more about you for myself.'

There was no time to wonder what he meant—she was hauled against the hard length of his body and his mouth was covering hers before she could draw breath. Swamped by blinding rage, she fought with everything in her but she managed only to wrench her head away. 'Don't!' She spoke with a fury she had not needed to use on Franz. 'Let go of me at once!'

Stirling's response was a short bark of laughter before he dipped his head and claimed her mouth again. And there was no escaping this time. One hand came up to the back of her head, holding her in place while he kissed her punishingly. There was no passion in it; there was only anger, an anger which seemed almost to match her own. Rebecca struggled, fighting for breath, able easily to ignore the feel of his body against hers, able easily to forget how often she had wanted to be held by him.

That was before his kiss changed, before the pressure of his mouth parted her lips fully to allow the shocking exploration of his tongue across the inside of her lower lip—and the small sound of protest she managed only made matters worse. Stirling seized the opportunity of plunging deeper, the movement of his tongue being nothing short of erotic now. The violence of his kiss had lessened and it kept on lessening until, quite suddenly, Rebecca was responding to it. She was kissing him back without even realising what she was doing, moving her body closer to his and revelling in the hardness of it, the strength of it. Her awareness of his arousal sent a flash of fire through her veins, drawing from her another sound, but not one of protest. She heard it as if from far away, the sensuous quality in it, the wanting in it ...

It was Stirling who stopped the action, his head lifting to look down at her with scepticism and triumph. 'Tell me about it,' he drawled. 'Is that how you fended off Schumacher?'

The humiliation Becky knew at that remark was more than she could cope with. She retaliated with a violence she had not known herself capable of. 'Damn you! No, it isn't.' Her right hand came up and she slapped him for all she was worth. 'But that *is* the way I fend off married men!'

Both of them gasped, Becky being doubly shocked by her actions as well as her words. In the sudden, awful silence which followed they stared speechlessly at one another.

Stirling put a hand to his face and turned away. 'So that's what it was about. I'm sorry, Rebecca. I tried several times to tell you but . . .' He turned back to look her directly in the eyes. 'I'm very sorry.'

So was she. She was almost sorry for him, he sounded so wretched. She felt like crying. It was a need so strong in her, she had to close her eyes and turn her head away, willing herself to composure. Perhaps it was perverse in the circumstances, but beyond everything else she was protesting inwardly about the conclusions he must have reached about her. Only minutes before, she had responded to him with unmistakable desire. He would be certain she was easy now, certain that she was what he had thought her in the beginning, when in her unthinking resentment of him at Heathrow she had deliberately given him the wrong impression. It was not possible to tell him that it was *his* kiss, the feel of his body that had made her respond so eagerly. No, it was not possible, nor was it necessary. After all, what did it matter now?

She walked away without another word and, this time, he made no attempt to stop her.

In the privacy of her room she cried, making no effort to stop the flow of tears. She believed it was healthy to cry, to give vent to all the emotions which had raged inside her for the entire evening. With the tears, the last of her anger ebbed away until she was able, if not to sleep, then at least to think clearly. To be fair, Stirling had tried to tell her, she knew that. There had been several times when he'd begun to and had changed his mind—or been interrupted. But again, what did it matter now?

She could only thank her lucky stars that she had found out he was married before she had become emotionally involved with him.

CHAPTER SEVEN

REBECCA woke with a start. She had been dreaming but the memory of it had already slipped away. A glance at her bedside clock told her it was almost eight—and what was she going to do with the long day ahead of her? What was she going to do about Stirling?

She closed her eyes and stayed where she was for the moment, wishing pointlessly that she had never been on that plane from New York to London. If she had only stayed another day or two with Michael McCaffrey... But such a wish was indeed pointless. What had happened had happened, and if she hadn't met up again with Stirling on the plane she would have met him here at the villa. How odd, how strange life was at times! It was as if she had been destined to meet him again, ten years on...

A groan escaped from her before a humourless smile tugged at her lips. What had she thought last night? That she could thank her lucky stars she had not become emotionally involved with Stirling? But that wasn't the case. Oh, she wasn't in love with him, as Ingrid insisted, but she was not exactly uninvolved, either. Not totally.

Slowly, like one many years older, she got herself out of bed—only to spot immediately the folded sheet of notepaper on the floor behind her door. It was from Stirling, written boldly in black ink.

Rebecca, I *must* talk to you. In private, obviously. I'm sure that neither of us would wish to involve

our hosts with any of this. Please come out with
me today, as we had intended. Stirling.

While showering she planned what to wear, just jeans
and a sweater; the day was not as fine as the previous
ones had been, and there was still a hint of last night's
rain hanging around. Somehow, that seemed
appropriate.

Whether Stirling had waited to hear the sound of her
door opening, she didn't know, but there he was in the
corridor when she emerged. She sighed inwardly, noticing
that he looked as unrested as she felt.

'Well?' That was all he said, no good morning, no
preamble.

Only fractionally did she hesitate. 'Yes, I'll come out
with you.'

His relief was palpable, confirming to her that she
was doing the right thing. It was important to him that
they talk. As for her—well, her own curiosity was
insisting on it. 'Then let's go down to breakfast together.' He reached for her arm but she side-stepped him,
saying she would be down after she had said hello to
Ingrid.

Nobody thought anything of it at breakfast, of course,
when Stirling and Rebecca got up to leave. In front of
everyone, he had asked her whether she would mind if
he called in at his house first.

'I'd been wondering about your house.' They were just
pulling away from the villa. The roof of the car was up
because it was still drizzling, and the atmosphere inside
the vehicle was a little tense.

'It's being decorated.'

'I know. I meant, I was wondering why you bought
a house here.'

'Why not?' Stirling shrugged. 'Like you, I love Lucerne, and you haven't seen the best of it. You should see it in the winter, be here when the snow's here, when there's skiing, festivals, music and lights adorning the streets.'

To say it was an idea that appealed to her would be an understatement, but she made no comment.

'Lucerne is also handy for commuting,' he went on. 'Not just to Berne and Zurich but from Zurich to any part of the world.'

'So your house here is your home? I mean, I wondered whether you had several.'

'I have; I have an apartment in London and one in New York. But my house here *is* home. You see the difference?'

'Of course I see the difference.' And home, here, was not where his wife was. But he was clearly not ready to talk about that just yet.

For Becky the day became strangely unreal as they continued to drive—in silence now. Stirling's house was just outside Stans, built in typically Swiss fashion; it was a chalet but it was huge and very handsome. She registered the flower boxes at the shuttered windows, spilling over prettily with vivid red geraniums; she saw the gardens and the man who was tending them, she saw the decorators inside and was hit by the strong smell of varnish with which they were treating the predominantly wooden walls. She saw the furniture covered in white sheets and sat on what she took to be a chair while Stirling talked to the men—but it was all somehow unreal. Later, she would be hard-pressed to bring the picture of the house back into her mind, gorgeous though it was.

'Ready?' Stirling appeared in the doorway. 'Sorry about the smell of varnish. Let's get out of here, shall we?'

They didn't get far. Stirling drove to the bottom of the sweeping driveway and stopped, turning to look thoughtfully at his property. He switched the engine off. 'I bought this place at a time of...at a time when I was particularly down. It was something of a sanctuary and— I suppose it still is.'

'A sanctuary?'

'From my marriage.' He turned to face her. 'A marriage which went drastically wrong, Rebecca. A marriage which still is drastically wrong.' He glanced away briefly, his fingers running raggedly through his hair. 'I did try to tell you, really I did—several times. The moment never seemed right. But it's no big deal, please believe that.'

'That's a matter of opinion,' she said coldly. 'I hate deceit. And it wasn't necessary.'

'I know, and I agree with you.' He shrugged helplessly. 'I can only apologise again. But I mean what I say, it isn't a big deal. I filed for divorce the day I met you, I mean when I met you on the plane from New York. I'd been with my lawyers there, hence my late arrival at the airport, whereupon I was immediately paged to the telephone. There was a lot to sort out...'

Becky heard all the words, and she registered them, but she also heard the unhappiness in his voice. It was written all over his face, too. He might have filed for divorce but divorce was not what he wanted, that much was obvious, and in spite of everything her heart went out to him. 'I'm...you have my sympathy, Stirling. I know divorce can be a shattering experience.'

'Shattering?' His laughter was hard, short, mirthless. 'It isn't shattering, it's a relief! Angel has given me nothing but pain—herself, too, for that matter.'

'Angel?'

His mouth twisted cynically. 'You might well wonder about that. An angel she is not. She was christened Angela but her professional name was Angel Dorsey.'

Angel Dorsey! Rebecca nodded slowly; she knew the name, and the face, very well. At least, she used to know the face, from magazine covers. Angel Dorsey had been one of *the* top models in the world; she was American, a blue-eyed blonde with that all-American image of beauty and a perfect, but perfect, figure to go with it. Yes, she could see at once why Stirling had remarked to Bruno on the similarity to Ingrid. 'I've heard of her. That is, I know the name but—well, I'd been under the impression that she'd just disappeared from the face of the earth.'

'Almost right.'

In an effort to mask the inexplicable pain she was suddenly feeling, she smiled. 'You mean she disappeared when she married you?'

'I mean she's no longer in the public eye, hasn't been for a long time.' With his earlier cynicism he went on, 'She remained very much in the limelight for at least two months after we married. Believe me, she did not let a little thing like marriage cramp her style, she carried on precisely as she had carried on before, with her career and with her...private life. Before her so-called commitment to me, and for the record I'm talking about the very *night* before, she was in bed with one of her lovers. Except that I didn't know about her lovers, not how numerous they had been, until *after*, not until she told me, not until the day I walked into our New York apartment and found her in bed with one of them. We'd been married almost eight weeks by then and it was over, right then and there.'

With that, he turned away to stare out of the window. Becky heard the sound of a car in the distance and the sound of Stirling's breathing as if it were all amplified. This, while at the same time there was a rushing noise in her ears.

Against her better judgement she did not tell him to take her back to the villa. Against her better judgement she wanted to help him. He was hurting like hell, he was hurting and she cared enough to want to help. Even though she couldn't, she wanted to try. With a brightness that sounded false even to her own ears, she suggested they press on. 'Let's go on to Engelberg, Stirling.'

He looked at her gratefully, putting the Corniche into gear and moving smoothly back on to the road.

For once, the scenery was lost on Rebecca. Her mind was spinning furiously with unanswered questions. Why had Angel married Stirling? How could she have behaved like that? She couldn't have loved him—so why marry him? A girl like that, she could have taken her pick of any man in the world.

The thought pulled her up short. She glanced over at Stirling and made a silent apology. Stirling Robard was not just any man, he was an extraordinary one. Against the odds he had made himself into a millionaire while he was still young. He was also devastating to look at, and this was not just Becky's opinion. More importantly there was a depth to him, a sensitivity that perhaps few people would guess at.

He had been quite a catch. He too could have taken his choice.

Well, he had. He had chosen Angel Dorsey—and Angel Dorsey had chosen him...and now there was a divorce in the making. Why only now? Why, if the rot had set in three years ago, so quickly after they had married, why were they only starting divorce proceedings now? Was this an American legal requirement, perhaps? Did one have to wait three years?

When they got to the restaurant in Engelberg, she asked him, waiting first until they were seated and their drinks had arrived.

'I would have divorced Angel long ago if she hadn't begged me not to,' he said.

Becky frowned. If that were true, it made the matter of his being married almost irrelevant, a technicality. But was it true? 'She begged you not to? So she does love you. I mean, she's still in love with you...'

He responded with laughter, again without mirth. 'Still? She never was in love with me. Believe me, Angel doesn't know the meaning of the word.'

They were interrupted by the appearance of a waitress and Becky gave her order without thinking about it. She was too distracted to care what she ate; she was alternating between wanting to run away from Stirling and doing what any friend would do: being a good listener. Giving him a shoulder to cry on might be the right thing—yet she was feeling extremely vulnerable for some reason. Perhaps she cared too much, more than she realised?

'Well,' she said when they were alone again, 'what else was I supposed to think? I mean, why have you only just decided to get divorced?' She looked straight at him, seeing the slate-grey eyes considering her. He was hesitant, so she added, 'If I'm prying, just say so. I don't want to do that.'

He smiled, reaching for her hand across the table. 'You're not prying. You're being kind and I appreciate it. I'm not reluctant to talk, Rebecca, it's just...that it's a sordid story.'

She blinked at that. 'Sordid? People are getting divorced every day of the year, Stirling. I don't think——'

'Then let me explain.' Briefly he turned away, as if gathering his thoughts. The rain was coming down heavily now and the mountains surrounding them were cloaked in low clouds. 'The night I met Angel, which was at a party in New York, one I almost didn't go to, she was a bit drunk, I mean giggly drunk.'

'So?'

He smiled. 'Yes, quite. I didn't think anything of it, either. I thought she was fun. What I didn't know...what I didn't know was that she had a drink problem. Believe me, if I had even suspected it, I'd have steered very, *very* clear of her!'

Becky nodded, understanding the sudden vehemence in his voice. His father. Stirling's father had drunk himself to death and—and what of Angel? What had happened? 'Did she know she had a problem?'

'Not at that stage, no. She didn't admit it for quite some time. It's a very insidious process, Rebecca...' He glanced away briefly, sighing. 'Anyway, I was only at the party for business reasons and I was bored. Meeting Angel changed that, although I must be honest and say that at first I couldn't see anything beyond her physical beauty. She was a stunner, and, believe it or not, it was out of character for me to meet a woman and bed her all on the same day. But that's what happened, we left together and ended up in bed together that night—and when she woke up the next morning she was very sober and very much down-to-earth. To start with, she asked me what my name was...'

He paused, waiting for Becky's reaction. Outwardly she didn't show one, inwardly she was asking herself whether she really wanted to hear this kind of detail. She said nothing.

'Rebecca, I know it sounds trite to describe my marriage as a mistake but that's what it was. Looking back, I can't imagine what I was thinking about. All I can say is that I was totally besotted by Angel, I asked her to marry me three days after I met her—and she said yes. During that short time, I never saw her touch a drink at all. I had heard her life story and I knew that despite the high-life she was used to, the money, the glamour, the friends, the fabulous holidays and all that, she was basically insecure and as lonely as hell. She'd come from a poor family in the mid-west, had no surviving relatives, and had made good as a model. She was in great demand professionally.'

Again he paused, toying with his wine glass before looking at Becky again. Then, as if to get it done with he said, 'What I didn't know was how much she was in demand in other ways, how many lovers she'd had, or about the ones she continued to see. It was only after we married, which was, as I said, very soon after I met her, that I discovered the extent of that—and the extent of her drinking. The latter happened in patches at first...I talked to her about it until I was blue in the face. It made no difference. She just laughed and called me "holier than thou". Even in the eight weeks our marriage lasted, her dependence on alcohol accelerated. She was aggressive or even violent at times and I knew there was big trouble on the horizon for her. I saw it coming and I hated the situation but I cared enough to be worried, very worried, because in some ways Angel is extremely childlike and vulnerable. I felt sorry for her, and I realised that I'd felt sorry for her from the start, crazy though that might sound. When I continued to hassle her about the booze, she insisted she could handle it, that she was "far" from being addicted. She didn't realise how far gone she was already...'

The sinking in the pit of her stomach told Becky that she already knew the answer to the question she was about to ask. At some level she knew, before she had time to work it out with her head, that Angel was currently experiencing the big trouble Stirling had anticipated.

But she was wrong about that. When she asked where Angel was now, she was surprised by the answer she got.

'Right now she's in Spain, she's in Puerto Banus—to the best of my knowledge, that is—staying at the villa of someone she describes as an old friend.' His smile was wry, his shrug an attempt to convince Becky that he really didn't care what his wife was up to. 'Many of her "old friends" are extremely wealthy men,' he went on, 'and Angel still—well, she is still a good-looking woman.'

'Of course she is.' Angel Dorsey had been in her early twenties when she was at the top of her profession, an absolute beauty, and she could only be in her late twenties now.

'There's no of course about it.' Stirling shook his head, his expression grim. 'The crazy thing is that part of her insecurity is her fear of getting older, fear of losing her looks.'

Again Becky nodded, this time with a sympathy that extended to Angel. 'It is ironic. I mean, in time the abuse of alcohol would be the very thing to precipitate that.'

'Exactly. And it needn't take that long, either. In the three years since I walked away from our marriage, Angel has had a rough time, very rough, the kind of experience that takes its toll—and this is why I've only just filed for divorce.'

Rebecca had watched him carefully without appearing to do so, and the pain she saw in his eyes now was all she needed to be sure of that which she already knew, in her heart. Whether Angel was drinking or not drinking, divorce or no divorce, Stirling was still in love with her. He was vulnerable...and so was she, Becky. In that moment, she knew what she had to do, and she had to do it as quickly as possible.

'Hi, Becky. You're back early, it's only just turned three.'

'I know. There was no point in our driving around in the rain. I—Ingrid, I have to leave. Here, I mean. Switzerland.'

Ingrid nodded; she had seen this coming. In all the years she had known Becky Hill, she had never, ever seen her so affected by a man. Heaven knew there had been plenty of them, very short-lived relationships which didn't even merit that description. She'd had more boyfriends than herself and the other two girls they lived with added together. This, because no one had ever lasted with Becky. She had found fault with them all. The strange thing was, it wasn't as if she had known what she was looking for in the first place—if, indeed, she had been looking for Mr Right. She had never expressed a desire to get married; on the other hand, she had never expressed a desire not to, either.

'Can't say I'm surprised to hear it.' Ingrid sighed inwardly. Well, it had finally happened. Whatever qualities Becky wanted in a man, she had found them in

Stirling Robard—but he was married. It seemed ironic. 'Did you have a fight? Did you tell him you know he's married?'

'Not today. Last night. Today we talked and——' Rebecca glanced away as she sat tiredly on the edge of Ingrid's bed.

'And?'

'And you were right, of course. It's by no means a healthy marriage. In fact, Stirling has filed for divorce.'

Ingrid sat upright, her hands opening expressively. 'So what's the problem? Why leave? In any case——'

Becky held up a hand, stopping her in mid-sentence. 'I'm too involved. I'm not in love with him, Ingrid, but if I stay in his space, there could be a possible danger of it.'

The other girl suppressed a smile. 'But you are involved—and he isn't. Right?'

'Sort of. Stirling is involved with his wife. Regardless of the divorce, he's still in love with her.'

'Becky! Are you *sure* about that?'

'I'm sure.' She sighed, shrugged, and looked at her friend bravely. 'Let me start by telling you who he married. Angel Dorsey.'

'Wow!' Ingrid was appropriately impressed, then, frowning, said, 'But that doesn't mean—I mean, I thought you told me he'd learned that beauty is only skin deep.'

'He has.' And Rebecca understood, now, why Stirling had hesitated as far as she was concerned, why there had been this holding back with her. It hadn't only been because he was married, it had been because he was physically attracted to her and he didn't want to be. He was wary of beautiful women, and who could blame him? 'And he learnt that the hard way, Ingrid. He's had a bad time with Angel but he loves her regardless. He said himself that she's childlike and vulnerable—and *that's* what appeals to him. He said he was besotted with her when he married her. What he doesn't seem to realise is that he still is.'

'So Becky's taking a graceful exit.'

'Becky's taking an exit while she's still detached enough to see that further involvement would be a road leading nowhere.' She reached for the telephone. 'What's the number of the airline—or will you ask directory enquiries for me, please?'

Fifteen minutes later, her seat booked on a flight the following day, Becky got to her feet and smiled. 'You know, you're looking much better. How are you feeling?'

'A bit better. Wish I were coming home with you, I'm starting to get bored. No, that's not true, I've been bored for days...'

'I'm not going home. Well, perhaps for a day, to collect some fresh clothes. I'm going to Colchester to see my parents.'

'Conscience getting to you?'

'No. I want to see them.' And she meant it. 'Speaking of which, parents I mean, I'm going down now to tell yours that I'm leaving.'

But she didn't do so immediately. Instead she went into her own room and took a shower. It wasn't that she particularly wanted one, it was that she needed time to rehearse what she was going to say to Bruno and Isabelle. Her departure would be abrupt, unexpected, and she had to make her reasons for leaving sound convincing. Moreover, she had to be especially careful as far as Stirling was concerned. He was going to assume that her sudden exit from the villa had something to do with him. It was going to be tricky convincing him to the contrary but, somehow, she had to.

CHAPTER EIGHT

IT WAS sunny in London. Becky reached her home in Hammersmith during the late afternoon undecided whether to drive to Colchester or whether to take the train. Undecided whether to leave tonight or in the morning. She would ring her parents, but not until she'd had a cup of tea.

There was no one else around and she sat, sighing, experiencing mixed feelings at having left Switzerland...the villa...Stirling. It had been the sensible thing to do, the only thing to do, yet she wondered how Stirling had reacted to the news. There had been no need for her to convince him that she was leaving simply because she wanted to. Fate had taken a hand. Fate or Lady Luck. By the time she had gone downstairs to talk to her hosts, Stirling had left for Berne. There had, Bruno had explained, been some sort of emergency in his office there. His staff had been trying to reach him on his car telephone—which had been switched off while he had been out with Becky.

The Bachmanns had been obviously puzzled at her abrupt departure, exchanging glances when she broke the news. But they had been far too tactful to say anything other than how sorry they were that she was leaving—and how much they would look forward to seeing her again.

Catching herself sighing again, she moved into action. Moping was pointless. Thinking it all through again, as she had on the flight home, several times, was also pointless. Missing him was pointless, too.

'Mum? It's me. Yes, I'm back in England. I want to come and see you... Yes, I know it's been four months. I know I don't live a million miles away. That's why I'm ringing, I want to come and see you...'

Within the hour she was on the road, driving her elderly but trustworthy Triumph, and feeling much better. At least she was doing something, going somewhere, and after a few days with her parents she would resume her work and get her life back on an even keel again. That was what she wanted—peace. So she would spend a few days with her parents, time enough in which to visit Ian and Susan and their families, both of whom still lived in Colchester. Vaguely, she wondered how Stirling felt about children. Had he wanted them? Did he like them, even? And what was she going to tell her family about him? Should she mention his being at the villa or not? She opted in favour—why not? In any case, there was always the chance of Ingrid mentioning him, not that she saw much of Becky's family, and it wasn't worth telling Ingrid never to mention his name. After all, there was nothing to hide.

As always, it was good to be home, for a few days at least. George and Elizabeth Hill were in their late fifties, young in outlook and devoted to one another. They doted on their grandchildren as well as their children and were easy to be with. But they were both worriers, they always had been, most especially where Rebecca was concerned. They wanted to see her settled rather than 'flitting here and there' and, while she was not averse to the idea, she sometimes found their questions about her love life, or rather her private life, rather irritating.

The mention of Stirling Robard, therefore, was more than enough to prompt a hundred questions.

Rebecca answered them all matter-of-factly, hesitating only when her parents wanted to know what had gone wrong with his marriage. 'That's hardly my business—or yours. All I can tell you is that he's in the throes of divorce. It seems his marriage was something of a mistake from the beginning. That was his word, by the way, not mine.'

It was the same with Ian and with Susan, whom she saw in their respective homes, although her brother seemed more interested in Stirling's professional success than in his marriage. With Susan it was the opposite. Becky began to regret having mentioned his presence at the villa at all, especially when her sister looked pointedly at her and asked how she had felt on seeing him again.

'Pleased, of course.' Becky had spent a couple of hours with Susan, catching up on all the news, and they were in the living-room. Her husband had not yet got home from work and the children were out in the garden playing. 'After all, he is an old family friend.'

'That wasn't your attitude when you phoned me from Heathrow, when you'd found yourself on the same plane.'

'No, well...' Rebecca was shifting uncomfortably in her seat, realising that she was doing so and feeling cross about it. 'What can I tell you? I was still associating him with the past then, wrongly so, of course.'

'And now?'

'What do you mean?'

'I mean how do you feel about him now?'

She tried not to hesitate. 'He's a very nice man.'

Susan smiled at that. 'He was always a looker. I told you, I used to be half in love with him. And you had an awful crush on him, didn't you?'

The younger girl tried to turn it all into a joke. 'I see, with you it was love, with me it was a crush, mm?'

'You were thirteen, I was twenty. Bit old to have a crush, as such. I think, if Alan hadn't come into my life, I'd have made a definite play for Stirling...'

At which point, Alan came in. He hadn't heard a word, happily, or further questions might have ensued.

Becky wasn't staying for dinner; she stayed only long enough to have a brief chat with her brother-in-law before leaving. The entire family were gathering at her parents' for lunch the following day, Sunday, so she would see more of them then.

When she got back to her parents' home there was still some daylight, though the streetlamps were lit. The clocks had been turned back—November was approaching but the weather was still quite mild. In the cul-de-sac in which her parents lived there were just two street lights and under one of them, right outside the house, a dark red Mercedes was parked. Rebecca eyed it with some puzzlement, wondering why a visitor would park there rather than on the drive, where there was plenty of room outside the double garages. Furthermore, who did they know who drove a spanking new Mercedes?

'We have a surprise for you.' Her father opened the door to her, smiling, his greying head nodding in the direction of the living-room. 'You'll never guess...'

Rebecca did guess. She said nothing, she was only glad of the few seconds of knowing, of warning, before she found herself face to face with Stirling. A few seconds in which she tried to compose herself. His turning up

here was the last thing she had expected and her heart
was beating idiotically fast. Probably from the shock,
she told herself. So much for her intention to get her life
back on an even keel!

As had always been the case in the past, he was thoroughly at home. Mum was fussing him, Dad was
beaming at him. And Stirling...he stood at once, looking
at Rebecca with a mixture of open admiration and, if
she was reading his eyes correctly, some mischief. She
was right about the mischief.

'Rebecca. I missed you. You ran away.'

'Don't be silly.' She managed a very natural smile, a
toss of her head. 'I told you I wanted to visit Mum and
Dad.' She turned to her parents laughingly. 'And precisely when did Stirling come and inflict himself upon
you?'

With good humour she was chided for that—while the
man in question laughed appreciatively.

'Stirling came a couple of hours ago, not long after
you'd left for Susan's,' her mother said, eyeing him as
if she were seeing a long-lost son. 'And it's been so nice.
We've been able to bring him up-to-date on all the family
news and everything.'

Briefly, Becky's eyes met with his and she groaned
inwardly, sympathising. She herself had brought him up-
to-date in Switzerland and she knew her parents would
have gone into much more detail. She caught his grin
and glanced away, not wanting to laugh herself.

'He wants to steal you from us,' George put in. 'Just
for the evening. He wants to take you out to dinner—
right, Stirling?'

'Right.' Again their eyes met, and Becky shook her
head.

'I don't think that's on, not when I'm here to visit you two.'

Stirling's smile was slow and knowing. 'Oh, I invited your parents to join us, I said we should all go out.'

'And I,' Elizabeth said, 'had a better idea. You young ones go out alone, provided Stirling stays the night and has lunch with us all tomorrow. That way, everyone gets to see everyone.' She finished quite proudly, looking at her daughter as if she expected a compliment.

Of course there was none forthcoming. It was all Rebecca could do to hide her annoyance. Stay the *night*? What was he doing here in the first place? 'I—well, you seem to have it all tied up, Mother. I just hope you didn't put Stirling on the spot,' she added, glancing at him. Everyone was seated except she, and her agitation was barely concealed. 'I mean, it might be very inconvenient for Stirling to stay here for the night.' She turned to him with more than a hint of defiance. 'I'm sure you'd rather be in your own apartment in town—there must be things you have to see to there.'

'On the contrary, it'll be a pleasure to spend the night here. It'll be like old times.'

'Exactly!' said George. 'The twin beds are still there in Ian's old room, nothing's changed. Nothing except us,' he went on, his smile taking in everyone.

'You can say that again, George.' Stirling spoke quietly, his eyes moving once more to Rebecca. 'Nothing except us, and some of us have changed quite drastically at that.'

'You ran away, Rebecca.'

'Nonsense.' They were in his Mercedes, heading...she knew not where. She had learned that Stirling had flown in to Heathrow around lunchtime that day and that this

car lived permanently in England. He had brought into
the house only a very small suitcase, a briefcase and the
suit he was now wearing. It was pale grey, worn with a
pale blue shirt and a silk tie. His blond hair was still
damp from the shower he'd just taken and the faint but
intriguingly male scent of his aftershave was reaching
her. 'I told you I wanted to see my parents.'

'No, you told me you ought to see them.'

'Well, that changed. It became a want rather than an
ought.'

'Really?' He glanced at her, smiling, his eyes flitting
over the length of her. She was wearing a simple woollen
midnight-blue shift dress with a matching jacket. It was
smart, plain and not particularly flattering to the figure,
although the look in Stirling's eyes indicated that he
thought to the contrary. 'Well, that's all right then.
Nevertheless, you could have stayed a few more days
before heading for your parents—and I believe you
wanted to. Didn't I manage to teach you anything about
giving yourself permission to do what you want to do?'

'Yes. But I'll tell you frankly that I suspect the rea-
soning on which that attitude is based. In your case, at
any rate.'

'Meaning?'

'I think in your case it's a sort of running away. I
think you please yourself, because you're in a position
to, but you're not really happy at all. You can give
yourself permission to ignore the oughts and the shoulds,
you can do that till the cows come home, but in your
case it is not going to make you happy.'

'Fascinating,' he said levelly. 'But what's all this about
"in my case", specifically?'

She didn't hold back. 'Specifically, Angel. Angel gave
herself permission to do what she wanted to do, which

included sleeping with someone the night before she married you. And after. And you hated it, obviously.'

Stirling didn't deny that. In fact he repeated 'Obviously,' before he glanced at her again. 'So?'

'So I think you've been running away ever since. From yourself, from your feelings. You're determined to do your own thing but it isn't making you happy.'

'Fascinating,' he said again, but he made no further comment and neither did Becky. She turned to look out of the window in the gathering darkness. They were heading east in the direction of Elmstead Market and she couldn't imagine where he had it in mind to have dinner.

It was Stirling who broke the silence. 'I like the way you speak your mind, Rebecca. I wanted very much to talk to you more, you know. That's why I'm here now.'

'I gathered that.'

He glanced at her again, frowning. 'Why are you being hostile about it?'

'I'm not. I'm—just surprised to see you, that's all.'

'If that's true, then I'm surprised to hear it. But it isn't true, is it? I think you know just as well as I do what's happening with you and me.'

Rebecca's head snapped round. If she had seen the look of alarm on her face, she might have laughed at herself. 'I—what do you mean? I haven't got the faintest idea what you're talking about.'

He laughed, unable to prevent it. 'Don't look so worried! I'm not a threat to you. We're friends, remember? I'm very fond of you, I always was—but there's a little more to it these days.'

'Like what?' She was still panicking inwardly.

'Like the fact that we're attracted to one another.'

With that, she looked away, aware that her cheeks were colouring and hating herself for it. 'You flatter yourself.'

He ignored that. 'And we didn't first feel the attraction in Lucerne, either. It was there the moment we looked at each other on that aeroplane, the instant we touched.'

Her head was still averted. She couldn't comment, wouldn't comment. He was right, she admitted to herself reluctantly, remembering how the touch of his hand had almost burned her, how in her resentment she had tried to tell herself it was abhorrent. Feeling obliged to say something, she threw in a *non sequitur*. 'Where are we eating?'

'We're just about there.' No sooner had he spoken than he turned off the road, followed a narrow lane for a few hundred yards then turned again into a car park at the back of an olde worlde pub which Rebecca had never even heard of. It was very welcoming and cosy with its log fires and lots of copper and brass, beautifully polished. They headed straight for the separate dining-room because they were hungry, opting to have a drink at their table rather than in the bar.

In spite of the pleasant surroundings, Becky was not at ease. She looked at Stirling and wondered why he was really here. What did he expect of her? True, they were friends, but for her there was more to it, and it was more than physical attraction. It scared her.

'Rebecca?'

'I—sorry. Gin and tonic for me. No ice.'

When the waiter went off with the drinks order, having left menus on the table, Stirling surveyed her openly, his eyes narrowing. 'You're uptight. Why?'

'No, not at all.' She tossed back her long mane and smiled at him. 'I'm not uptight, I'm just hungry!'

They ordered smoked salmon to be followed by chateaubriand with a selection of vegetables, and it was not until the second course was almost finished that Stirling told her she had been wrong earlier. Until then they had talked about matters impersonal, which had put Becky entirely at her ease.

'Wrong? I was wrong about what?'

'About my running away, from myself, my feelings. And about my being unhappy. Although,' he added with a gentle smile, 'I have to say, since meeting you I've realised that something has been missing. I hadn't realised it, but I had been a little lonely.'

His words, and the way he reached for her hand, were enough to create a knot in Becky's stomach. She withdrew her hand, reaching for her wine glass. She even managed a laugh. 'Which is entirely of your own making. There need be no shortage of friends in your life—of either sex.'

'There are friends and friends,' he pointed out. 'Oh, I haven't been celibate these past three years, but there has been no one I could talk to, really talk to, about— things.'

'About Angel.'

'Not necessarily. Well, yes, but not only that. I mean about anything and everything, life, all sorts of things. For several years there hasn't been anyone I could talk to... how can I put it?... spontaneously, the way you and I do. I missed that. Especially with a woman. Do you know something? I never, ever, had a real conversation with Angel.'

Angel. There she was again. 'Tell me more about her.'

He shrugged. 'There's little else I can tell you. Suffice it to say I had to bail her out of trouble on numerous occasions.'

'No,' she persisted, 'that won't do. You've told me so much, tell me all of it. What kind of trouble? With the drinking?'

'Yes.'

'Did she need money? I mean, it must have affected her career——'

'She needed help, Rebecca. And, yes, she's needed money, support of various kinds, but most of all she needed professional help. I—she always turned to me, she said she still regarded me as her "best friend" no matter what had happened between us, she said she needed me regardless, and, though our marriage had ended after two months, she begged me not to divorce her. Well, to begin with it made no difference to me—whether we were legally divorced, I mean. There was no other woman in my life and I was in no hurry, I was as free as a bird as far as I was concerned.'

They were interrupted by the appearance of the waiter. Stirling ordered coffee and brandy for them both, turning, once they were alone, to reach for Becky's hand again. 'You're a good listener, my lovely.'

She glanced away but she did not withdraw her hand this time. 'You needed to get it all off your chest.'

'No, that isn't quite accurate. I wanted to talk about it not just for me but for you, too. I wanted to be honest with you, to tell you everything.'

'And I appreciate that, I respect it.'

'I wanted you to know that I have seen Angel during the past three years. Somehow she always managed to locate me when she was at rock bottom.'

'And you couldn't refuse to help her.' It was not an accusation or derision, it was a simple statement of fact.

'No, I couldn't.' He looked straight into her eyes then, and there was no apology in his. 'When all was said and done, I had married her. Again, it might sound trite in the circumstances, or at least strange to you, but when I went through the marriage ceremony I meant what I said. I believed I loved her.'

She nodded, knowing he had played down the last part of his story. It was not difficult to guess at the kind of rocky road Angel had travelled these past few years. So her initial reaction in Switzerland had been right after all: Angel had met with big trouble and Stirling had helped her. But of course he had. Hadn't he helped her, Becky, when she had been an ugly duckling, anti everything and everyone? So of course he would care about his wife, it was his nature. To say the least of it, he hadn't stopped caring either.

'The time came,' he went on, 'when I finally managed to persuade her to get professional help. She went into a private clinic and she got dried out. I only hope it lasts, but that's up to her. I've filed for divorce and, as far as I'm concerned, she's on her own now. If it does last, if she keeps off the booze, then the sordid story has a happy ending,' he added, his smile not altogether convincing. 'Now, that's quite enough about her and it's quite enough about me. I want to know more about you, Rebecca. Tell me more.'

She couldn't help laughing. 'I think I've told you all there is to know. Really I have!'

'Not true. What are the important things in life to you?'

She had to think about that. 'My work.' She didn't know what else to say.

'You find it fulfilling?'

'Fulfilling? Well, I do enjoy it.' She added the last sentence thoughtfully, silently acknowledging that it was not quite the same thing.

'So would you describe yourself as being happy?'

'Yes.' It came out just a little too quickly and inwardly she was questioning her answers. Happy, yes—all in all. Fulfilled? Well, more or less...

'Go on,' Stirling persisted. 'I think there was a "but" in there somewhere. What's missing? What is it you would like but haven't got in your life?'

'Nothing,' she said stubbornly, refusing to be drawn.

Stirling glanced down at the table before turning to signal for the bill, wondering why he had the strong feeling she was holding back from him. She never talked about herself unless prompted—and there was something she wasn't saying now.

'Are you bored?' he said suddenly, startling her.

'What?' Rebecca frowned, wondering why such an idea had sprung into his mind. 'Bored? In what way? With my life, you mean?'

'No.' He glanced around. 'This place. Tonight. Me.'

'Don't be silly.' Her laughter and her protest were genuine, he could see that. 'I've had—am having—a lovely time.'

Seeming satisfied, he nodded, paid the bill, and helped her into the jacket she had shed. They drove home at a leisurely pace, in a comfortable silence.

Her parents were in bed when they got back to the house. Stirling took Becky's key, opened the front door and suggested they had some coffee before they turned in. 'Shall I put the kettle on? Unless your mother's had a complete changeabout, I can probably remember where things live in the kitchen.'

'I'll come with you. It's all been modernised. Mum and Dad had a new kitchen put in about two years ago—so you won't find anything without an effort.'

They moved around quietly, saying nothing, until Stirling picked up where their earlier conversation had left off. 'I can't say the same thing myself.'

She turned to look at him, frowning. 'What?'

It was with some deliberation that he explained himself. 'I can't say there's nothing missing from my life—as I told you earlier.' He moved to where she was standing, his arm going around her waist as he drew her close. 'Take you, for instance. Finding Rebecca Hill in my life again has given me a great deal of pleasure, just in case you didn't realise it . . .'

'I—didn't realise it.' She almost stammered the words, unable to be sure he meant what he'd said, aware of the warning bells clanging in her head. She warned herself to be careful, very, very careful. If she didn't keep him at bay this time she would be tarred with the same brush as Angel; it had already been to her disadvantage that she, too, happened to be a model, and a very beautiful one, to use his own words. Moreover, she had no illusions about his feelings for Angel—or about his feelings for her. She was little more than a sympathetic listener to him, one he would no doubt take to his bed if she showed even the slightest willingness. And he already thought her easy, didn't he?

'Well, you better believe it.' He smiled down at her and, seeing what was coming, she stepped smartly backwards, away from him, telling him that she did not exist in order to give him pleasure. 'You or any other man,' she added. 'That's chauvinistic talk and I dislike it intensely.'

Merriment was the last thing she expected. He laughed, his eyes positively roguish as they slid over the length of her body. His next words confirmed all she had just thought, although he was still smiling, agreeing she did not exist for his pleasure. 'However, I don't think my remark was chauvinist. I was telling you the truth, I find you delightful in every way. What's chauvinist about that? You like me, too, obviously. Why else would you have spent so much time with me?'

'You didn't give me much choice tonight.'

'So you *were* bored.'

He seemed taken aback, so she apologised, realising how ungracious she must have sounded. 'Sorry, I didn't mean it that way. Of course I like you,' she added lightly. She turned to pour boiling water on to the coffee, afraid that her eyes might reveal just how much she liked him.

Again he stepped closer, this time cornering her because her back was against the sink-unit. He didn't touch her, he just stood right in front of her, impossibly tall and handsome, looking down into her emerald eyes. 'And what about the rest of it, Rebecca?'

She held his gaze and lied in her teeth. 'You were wrong about that. As I said, I like you—but that's as far as it goes. Physically, you're not my type.'

One eyebrow rose sardonically. 'Is that a fact?' Stirling moved away from her, sensing her alarm. What was she afraid of? Why was she lying? He backed off. The last thing he wanted to do was upset her in any way. 'Come on, let's drink this in the living-room, shall we?' He picked up the mugs and nodded for her to precede him, his eyes drawn inexorably to the swing of her hips as she walked.

Becky sat in her father's armchair, feeling tense again. He hadn't believed what she'd just told him, she was well aware of that. But he had changed his mind about kissing her and she didn't know whether she was glad or sorry about that. How perverse, she thought humourlessly, how perverse can I get? She glanced at him, only to find he was smiling faintly, his grey eyes gentle on her as he took the other armchair—well away from her. 'I don't take my happiness or my pleasures at someone else's expense, Rebecca.'

Which was precisely what his wife had done. She nodded. 'It never occurred to me that you would.' But what was he getting at?

'I worked very hard for a lot of years, fanatically so, obsessively so, but my priorities in life are different now. As I told you that day on the mountain, money has not made me happy, not of itself. As soon as I woke up to that fact, it lost its importance and I looked around for something that would—which is probably the main reason I rushed into marriage with Angel. Well, that was a mistake and a half! Anyway, I just take each day as it comes now, and maybe it is hedonistic but I do try to please myself these days, and I make no apology for that.'

'Nor should you,' she agreed.

'But as I say, I don't take my happiness at other people's expense.'

'No. But why are you making a point of this?'

'Because I want you to know it, to be sure of it. Because I want to see you again—and again and again.'

Rebecca looked at him steadily, her calm expression successfully hiding her inner feelings. Everything in her leapt at the prospect . . . but what should she say? She told herself her head must rule, that to continue seeing Stirling would be asking for trouble, trouble of the emotional kind, in a big way.

In the face of her silence he added softly, 'I do spend a lot of time in London, you know. And we are friends . . . so may I ring you? In a few days?'

Becky drained what was left of her coffee, mind whirring, heart thumping. With an ease and elegance she had to struggle for, she got to her feet. 'Of course,' she said casually, 'but I'm not making any promises, Stirling.'

CHAPTER NINE

STIRLING left during the late afternoon the following day, after a somewhat riotous lunch with the family, all of whom were still there when he went.

Becky saw him to his car. 'I'll ring you,' he said. 'Unfortunately I have to go to Paris in the morning—but only for a couple of days.'

She nodded and went back indoors, only to be met with a welter of questions.

'Are you going to see him again, Rebecca?'

'Is he going to ring you?'

'He seems awfully fond of children, doesn't he?' This, from her mother. 'I don't suppose he had time to have any with his wife...just as well.'

'When's he going to contact you?' This, from Susan, with a knowing look.

'I don't know.'

And then there was her brother's, 'Be careful, Sis. I'm not convinced he's got over his wife yet...'

Which makes two of us, Rebecca thought worriedly. Well, she could always say no when he did ring her.

Except that he didn't ring her. She left Colchester the following morning, calling in personally at her agency before going home to Hammersmith. She was available for work again and there was plenty around.

When she got to the house it was to find that Ingrid was back. She looked well and she was eager to hear all the news. 'I knew he'd be hot on your trail when you left Lucerne. It didn't take him long, did it? He was in

130

Berne for three days, as it turned out, and when he got back and learned that you'd disappeared he was obviously put out. He didn't try to hide it.'

Becky listened with interest. 'I don't know what he expects of me...'

'Expects? Don't get too heavy about it, just enjoy it for what it is.'

'That's just the problem, I don't know what it is.'

The entire week passed and there was no telephone call. Becky began to think he had changed his mind about seeing her again. She tried to tell herself it was just as well, because her disappointment was such that it forced her to acknowledge how very much she cared about him. She missed him dreadfully.

It was on Saturday morning that he turned up on the doorstep. Becky heard the doorbell and wished someone else would answer it. It wasn't even ten o'clock—and all four girls lay in on Saturdays when they could. Patti and Janice, she knew, would be dead to the world—and Ingrid hadn't slept at home last night.

Resignedly she got up, only to find Stirling standing there. He was smiling and her idiotic heart started racing again, her eyes feasting on him, taking in every detail from the blond hair to the smart navy blue overcoat he was wearing, under which was a navy cashmere sweater, to the black trousers and shoes. He looked expensive, just as he had when she had first seen him on the plane from New York. He was dressed for late October England, warmly but elegantly.

'I'd appreciate it if you'd invite me in,' he grinned. 'This isn't the warmest weather I've ever experienced!'

Rebecca laughed, shivering, feeling incredibly happy to see him and more than a little annoyed at the same time. She led the way indoors, pulling her housecoat closely around her. It was far from being a seductive garment; it was very much the sort of thing her mother would wear, practical and warm.

'Put the kettle on,' she said, sitting heavily at the kitchen table, watching him do her bidding. He slipped out of his overcoat and sat opposite her, grinning like a Cheshire cat. 'I missed you.'

'In a pig's eye.' She was determined not to let her pleasure at his words show. Besides, how could she believe him? 'Is that why you've been on the telephone every day?'

He frowned. 'Every day? I—but I did call on Tuesday, to explain that I wouldn't get back till late last night.'

'You did?'

'I spoke to someone called Patti. I assumed she was one of your cohabitants, if that's the right word? She does live here, doesn't she?'

'She does.' Indeed she did, and she was scatter-brained. And she had *not* passed on Stirling's message.

'She didn't tell you.' Stirling looked as cross as Becky felt. He got up. 'Tea or coffee?'

'Tea. The cups are in the cupboard near your left shoulder.'

'Well, I'm sorry, Rebecca. It never occurred to me that Patti wouldn't tell you about my call.'

What could she say? 'It's OK. It's not your fault.' And Patti was in for a telling-off in no uncertain terms! 'I—how was Paris?'

'I don't know, I only saw the inside of my office and my hotel room.' He turned to look at her. 'Did you miss me?'

'Of course not. Don't flatter yourself.'

'Maybe I am at that. Maybe you have so many blokes calling you that Patti didn't bother. She might have thought "What's one more or less?" for all I know.'

'She might at that.' Becky enjoyed the banter, she also enjoyed the way their eyes met with amusement and appreciation.

'You look beautiful,' he said suddenly, the smile fading from his mouth. 'And before you protest, I mean it. Have you just got out of bed?'

'Yes, you did wake me up.'

'I'm not going to apologise.'

'You never do.'

'Not true. Rarely but not never.'

It was her turn to grin. She was fighting a losing battle, wasn't she? In more ways than one.

'Will you have lunch with me, Legs?'

'*Legs?* Now how did you ... ?'

'Patti. She did *say* she would be sure to give "Legs" the message...'

'I see.'

'So? Lunch? And dinner tonight? And will you spend all day with me tomorrow? After all, we are friends...'

Rebecca was laughing openly now. 'Mmm. And I have never, ever, known anyone as manipulative as you.'

'Does that mean yes or does it mean no?'

'Do you often travel from country to country to carry on talking to a person?'

'No, not often. Well, Legs?'

She hesitated until she could hesitate no longer, wanting, childishly perhaps, to keep him on tenterhooks as long as possible, and battling, too, common sense versus heart. But she had known minutes ago which one had won yet again. So she said yes, she would have lunch with him. 'But that's all I'm committing myself to. Lunch—not necessarily dinner as well.'

They had lunch and they had dinner and she spent the following day with him, but she refused point blank when he suggested they went back to his apartment to spend Sunday evening. Instead they ate at a Chinese restaurant in Hammersmith and when the evening came to a close he drove her home and went inside to meet Patti and Janice. It proved to be one of those nights, however, when there wasn't only Ingrid and the other two girls there but various friends as well, and lovers. It was often like that, the house being inundated with people—and not for the first time did Becky wish that it weren't. Again she thought how nice it would be to have her own place, and peace, but this time she thought it more wistfully, to the point where she began to think seriously of doing something about it—though it would mean being unable to save as much money as she was currently saving.

Stirling left at around one in the morning and Becky went to bed, hoping that no one would take it into their head to start playing music. She had a heavy Monday ahead of her and she needed her sleep.

'Are you working on that tights commercial today, Becky?'

'Yes.' She looked at Ingrid with a smile. It was six-thirty on Monday morning and it was not their favourite time of day. 'You look rough, Ingrid. Let me pour you some tea.'

'Thanks. And thanks for the compliment, too! Too much wine last night... Are you seeing Stirling tonight?'

'No. He wanted to see me but I said no, I said I'd see him on Wednesday. I'm—trying to keep detached.'

Ingrid rolled her eyes. 'Detached? Is that how you do it? By denying yourself the pleasure of his company for a couple of nights? You're nuts!'

Maybe she was, because Wednesday took a long time to come and, by six-thirty that evening, Rebecca was dressed and ready and agitated. Stirling wasn't due until seven but she could hardly wait. They were going to the theatre, to a new musical which had recently opened in the West End.

He arrived on the stroke of seven, looking marvellous in a dark suit and overcoat. His eyes took in every detail of her appreciatively. She was wearing a dress he had seen before, in Switzerland, a simple black cocktail dress with a low neckline. Seeing the look in his eyes, she began to think she'd made a mistake in wearing it. He might have seen the dress before but he hadn't feasted his eyes on the swell of her breasts the way he was doing now...

'You're going to need a coat.' That was all he said.

'Of course. Is it very cold?'

'The temperature's dropped considerably since this afternoon.'

Janice came into the hall. 'Hi! Thought I recognised the voice. Come and have a quick drink while Becky's getting herself together.'

'I am together.' Rebecca smiled inwardly; it wasn't difficult to see that Janice wouldn't say no to an evening with Stirling Robard. He declined her offer politely and two minutes later he was seeing Becky into his car.

The show was dreadful. They left during the interval, pulling it to pieces and laughing over it. 'It won't last a month,' Stirling said. 'I'm surprised it's survived this long. What about that lead singer? Where do you suppose they dug him up from?' He took her arm and tucked it under his own as they headed back to the car. 'Now. Supper. Fancy anything in particular?'

'Hmm. Italian, I think.'

'Italian it is. In that case, we don't need the car.' He led her away from Shaftesbury Avenue, down a side street, saying he knew just the place.

There was nobody at home when they got back to the house. Becky could hardly believe it. 'In all the time I've lived here, except when the others have been on holiday, I think this has only happened to me twice. At this time of night, I mean. Coffee?'

'I'd love some.' Stirling followed her into the kitchen, laughing to himself.

'What's the joke?'

'The way you said "It's only happened to me twice." I don't know what to make of that.'

She was filling the kettle, standing with her back to him. 'Well, the place is normally like a mad house, as you must have noticed. I've been thinking seriously about getting my own place, if only to get some peace. It's what I'd planned to do eventually but——' The feel of his arms coming around her made her gasp. 'Don't!' The word came firmly but he didn't seem to know what she meant.

'What?'

'I said don't do that.'

She was turned around to face him—and he didn't let go of her. 'Why ever not? And why so vehement? What's the matter?'

'I—I'm sorry if I snapped, but I don't want this——'

'Why?' His smile was slow and knowing. 'Because physically I'm not your type?'

Colour flooded her face; it made her angry with herself as well as with him. 'Look, Stirling, I like you very much but that's all there is to it. There's nothing more than that——'

'But you were lying when you said I'm not your type. You have a short memory, Rebecca.' And with that she was pulled closely against him.

She struggled against the embrace not frantically but with some semblance of dignity—or so she hoped. 'Don't!' She began her standard rejection routine—going straight into phase two. 'Please, Stirling, let's just keep this on a friendly basis and then no one will get offended.'

He didn't even credit her line with an answer. He got on with kissing her instead, his mouth claiming hers inexorably as he shifted his stance so she was wedged between himself and the sink behind her. There was nothing she could do but be kissed, nothing she could do but fight it, and him, with her mind. Under no circumstances would he get a response this time; there would be no arousal in her whatever!

With pathetic determination she thought of other things, of anything except what he was doing to her.

But it didn't work. Everything was to his advantage. She was held in such a position that she was able to feel the entire length of him against her. His own arousal was immediate, giving her at once a heady sense of power—and of alarm. The latter increased when she felt the acquiescence of her own body, the heat surging through her veins, an ache of desire that began in the pit of her stomach. Against her own will she was moulding herself to him even as the voice in her head screamed its protest. It was loud enough to be heard, though, and when Stirling shifted his lips to her throat she moved, raising her head as she spoke to him angrily.

'For heaven's sake, stop this! How many times do I have to tell you? This is not what I want...'

Still he took no notice of her. One long-fingered hand slid around to her breast, making a liar out of her without the need for words. She was shaking, only too aware of the tell-tale signs of her body. She lowered her eyes, unable to look at him, a sob catching in her throat at the precise moment he spoke.

'I think I've proved my point...hey, what is it? Rebecca, look at me. What's the matter?'

'I——' It was all she could manage.

'Rebecca, please, what is it?' It sounded like genuine concern, which served only to make her want to cry all the more.

She shook her head. 'Leave me alone, Stirling, please.'

Very quietly he said, 'Look at me. Come on, we've had more than our share of misunderstandings. There's some kind of miscommunication going on here. I want to clear it up.'

Defiantly she raised her head and looked straight at him. 'All right. Yes, you proved your point. I am attracted to you—but only with my body.'

'Only?'

'You think there's no more to attraction than that? I thought you'd learned a few things over the years? Well, take it from me, there's much more to it—at least to the kind of relationship that interests me. Now move away from me, please.'

He didn't. She despaired that he ever would. 'I don't understand, we have a heck of a lot going for us. It isn't just...I see...or I think I do. Are you resisting because I'm married?'

'Married,' she repeated. 'Yes, you are, and I haven't forgotten it.'

'But I thought I'd made it clear that that's a mere detail.'

He had done that—but there was a lot more to it than the fact that he was still married, detail or no. Angel's unfaithfulness had damaged him more than he realised; it had coloured his opinion about at least one category of women in the world. Or did he come on this strongly with every female he was attracted to? She decided to ask him. 'Do you always come on this strongly, Stirling? Or am I especially privileged?'

Her cynicism was not lost on him. 'What do you mean by that?'

'Just what I say.'

'I don't usually meet with such resistance, not when the attraction is as strong as it is between us.'

She laughed because she couldn't help it. Oh, well, she had expected a straight answer and she'd got one!

'I don't see what's funny. I might add that this doesn't happen often; I'm no womaniser, I'm by no means easily pleased, in fact. But I am a normal, red-blooded man and you——' He paused, still unsmiling, unapologetic. 'You are one hell of a turn-on.'

That, as far as Becky was concerned, was the end of the discussion. 'I'd like you to go now.'

'Wait a minute——' His hand snaked out to cover her arm.

She looked at it pointedly. 'Goodnight, Stirling.' What would it take to get through to him? There was a glimmer of amusement in the grey eyes now, damn him!

'You can climb down from that high horse. What on earth is wrong with my kissing you? We're friends, aren't we? We've been having fun—what would be so wrong about adding a new dimension to that fun?'

Nothing, she thought, for you. From your point of view that's all it would be—fun. A transitory pleasure. But not for me. Oh, no, Stirling, you can't lure me to your bed that way, not with those lines. I've heard them all before.

'A hundred times,' she said, putting boredom into her voice.

'What?'

'That sort of thing, I've heard it a hundred times before, believe me.'

'I do believe you.'

'And flattery will get you nowhere.' Her green eyes flashed angrily. 'There's something you've yet to learn about me—I too am not easily pleased, not by any means. I too have a normal, healthy body, but it does not rule my head. *I* rule my life,' she added finally, tapping her temple and hoping she was telling the truth.

There was small triumph in his letting it—and her— go at that. He stepped away from her with a look of unconcealed interest, intrigue, on his face, his smile slow to start but devastatingly attractive when it grew.

Becky walked gracefully out of the kitchen, her head held high. The coffee had been forgotten and she was on her way to bed, or so she thought.

'Oh, no, Rebecca. I'm not going, and I'm certainly not going to leave things like this.' Very firmly he got hold of her and turned her round. 'You are going into the living-room. I am going to bring the coffee in. You are going to tell me what's really bugging you—and I am going to listen.'

She was unsure what to do. His attitude told her he meant business and he didn't let go of her until he had steered her to an armchair.

Resignedly she sat, taking the few seconds while he was out of the room to decide what to say. The truth would be the best thing. It always was.

'Well, Rebecca?'

She looked straight at him. 'I don't want to have an affair with you.'

'Why not?'

She shook her head. 'No. I owe you nothing, I don't owe you an explanation, you don't have to be privy to my reasons. That's my business.'

Stirling thought about that. He considered her words and felt at a loss to understand her. In Switzerland her physical messages had been different, there was no mistake about that—until she had learned he was married. But his marriage was a technicality, soon to be ended, and she knew that, so why was she behaving like this? In effect she had told him to keep his hands off her. Why? At length he said, 'OK. I accept that you have your reasons. And I accept that you don't want to share them with me.' What else could he say? If he pushed the point, he might be in danger of losing her, and that was the last thing he wanted. Maybe things would change when the divorce came through...

'So if an affair is what you're expecting of me——'

'Wait a minute.' He held up a hand. 'That's not fair. I'm not *expecting* anything of you. I never have. But I do want to go on seeing you...'

'And I'm beginning to think that's a very bad idea.' Beginning? She had thought so all along. The trouble was, when you loved someone... Briefly her eyes closed. Loved? Yes, she was in love with him, God help her!

'Rebecca?'

Her eyes came open. 'I'm—it was just a train of thought.'

'To which, again, I'm not going to be privy?'

'That's right.'

'Then perhaps you'd better tell me what you expect of me.'

'Nothing.'

He sighed. Inwardly he sighed even further. He got to his feet. 'All right, I'll say goodnight.'

To her astonishment he walked out. As the living-room door closed behind him, she stared at it. What did this mean? He hadn't said he would ring, he hadn't asked if he might...so was this the end? Had he taken what had, after all, been a very strong hint?

As the front door closed, her eyes closed. She spoke to the empty room, feeling panic stricken. 'Oh, lord, I hope not. I hope not!'

CHAPTER TEN

FOR three days Becky agonised, wishing she hadn't been so aggressive in her attitude. Why couldn't she just have enjoyed her relationship with Stirling for what it was, as Ingrid had advised? There again, it had to be better this way, better to finish it now before... before what? Before she became more emotionally involved? She could hardly be more emotionally involved.

He telephoned on the Saturday morning, not too early. In fact Becky was in the bath, it was Janice who took the message. The other girl hammered on the bathroom door. 'Becky? Stirling's on the phone. Do you want to call him back or shall I tell him to hang on?'

'I'll call him back. Take the number.' There was no hesitation, only a profound sense of relief.

He was at his apartment. She had begun to wonder whether he'd left London. 'Stirling? How are you?' Her casual friendliness amazed her. Inwardly she was shaking.

'I've just had a call from your mother, Rebecca.'

'My *mother*? I didn't know she had your number.'

'Of course. I gave it to her when I was there. She rang to ask...' there was a pause before, '...to ask whether I would like to spend Christmas there.'

Becky frowned. She had? But she had said nothing to her, Becky, about this. And they had only chatted a few days ago. Of course, she had talked about Stirling and how they were seeing one another... 'So what did you say?'

'I asked if I might let her know a little nearer the time.'
There was another pause. 'After all, Christmas is six or
seven weeks away.'

'Well, that's true.'

'And life has a way of presenting us with any number
of surprises, doesn't it? Planning is all very well; it works
some of the time but by no means all of the time.'

'You can say that again.'

'Ahh! I hear a smile in your voice. Am I right?'

'Spot on.'

'Are you doing anything today? Can you have lunch
with me?'

'I've just stepped out of the bath. Can you give me
an hour?' She put the phone down and floated back to
her room. The upstairs phone was on the landing, which
was sensible. With four females in the house it would
have been a bit silly to have an extension in any one of
the four bedrooms.

A moment later Ingrid came in. She took one look at
Becky's face and started laughing. 'Janice tells me that
was Stirling on the phone. Didn't surprise me. I knew
he'd ring. So what's the latest?'

'You knew? You felt certain?'

'Of course. He was just leaving you to stew for a few
days. Can't say I blame him after your little outburst
on Wednesday. Honestly, Becky, you really would be
easier on yourself if you just let things happen. I mean,
fancy telling a bloke point-blank that you don't want to
have an affair.'

That was met with indignation. 'I don't see why not!
Saves misunderstandings later on—and heaven knows
we've had our fair share of those. In any case, an affair
was what he wanted.'

'Wants, dear heart. Present tense. You don't think that'll have changed, do you? Hell's bells, how naïve can you get?'

All the pleasure left Rebecca's face. She sat down on her bed and looked helplessly at her friend. 'I don't know. I don't know why I accepted just now—he's coming for me in an hour.'

'You accepted because you're in love with him.' Ingrid waited for the denial. It never came.

'I—can't seem to behave sensibly where he's concerned.'

'It's often the way.' Ingrid was frowning, wondering how she could advise Becky without being ruthless. 'Look, love, if you happen to be thinking in terms of marriage——'

'I'm not.'

'Well, permanence then——'

'I'm not. Oh, he's come to terms with his disastrous marriage, true, but I know without doubt he wouldn't want to try it again, or anything like it, not after his experience. In any case, he's still in love with Angel—which makes me an even bigger fool.'

Ingrid sighed. 'I'd better leave you to get ready. Time's marching on.' She paused at the door, turning back to look at her friend. 'If there's anything I can say or do to help—just let me know.'

'There isn't. But thanks. I love you for that.'

'I love you, too.'

It was Ingrid who let Stirling in when he came. By then Patti and Janice had gone out shopping and Becky was not quite ready. When she walked into the living-room where the other two were, there was an abrupt, sudden silence. The atmosphere wasn't unpleasant but... it was one of those moments when one knows something has been said. About oneself. Becky looked quickly towards Ingrid—whose face was impassive.

'Ready?' Stirling was on his feet. She couldn't read his expression, either, but he seemed preoccupied. He walked briskly to the door, his hand on her arm, but he said nothing further until they were inside his car. 'How hungry are you, Rebecca?'

'To tell you the truth, not very.'

'Same here.' His look was a challenge and she tensed inwardly, wondering what was coming. 'Then will you come to my apartment and have something simple, an omelette or something? I want to talk to you.'

For long seconds she hesitated, confused. Something *had* been said just now. 'All right. Provided that's——'

'For goodness' sake! Yes. That's *all*. Lunch and a talk and that's *all*. All right?'

She stared at him in amazement. Never, ever, had he raised his voice like that. Something had upset him, that was for certain.

As soon as they got indoors, he came out with it. He didn't offer to show her around but it came as no surprise that his apartment was immaculate, very tastefully decorated and furnished—with a number of antique pieces blending in nicely.

Becky sat on a pale grey sofa covered in velvet, wondering what to expect.

'Can I get you something to drink?' Stirling hadn't sat, he was clearly agitated.

'No. I'd rather you told me what's on your mind.'

'You're a fine one to talk!' he exploded, staring down at her as if he might just take it into his mind to spank her any minute. 'If you had told me what's been on *your* mind, I could have cleared up an illusion I didn't even know you were labouring under.'

'I—like what. What are you talking about?'

'Ingrid. I make no apology. I know how close you two are—so I just asked her if she would be a friend to me, too, and tell me why I can't seem to get anywhere with you. She told me that you believe I still love Angel.'

'But it's true.' Becky knew no anger, either with Stirling or with Ingrid. She had been about to point this out to him for his own sake soon, in any case. 'And please don't bother to deny it.'

'I've never heard anything quite so ridiculous. Love her?' The words came quietly, which made them all the more convincing. His earlier agitation had gone. In fact he smiled a little. '*Love* her? I never loved her. Oh, I *thought* I was *in* love with her—please note the difference—but it wasn't even that. I was in love with a beautiful face, a beautiful body. I was in love with making love to that body. Why do you look shocked? You're good at speaking your own mind—most of the time. Or is it that you don't like what you're hearing?'

Becky looked away. Oh, if only he knew how much she liked it! Was it true? Had he only been in love with love? Was that what he was saying? She looked at the broad expanse of his back. He was standing at a cocktail cabinet, pouring a neat whisky. Drinking spirits was out of character for him and she frowned.

He saw it and misunderstood it. 'Why the frown? Damn it, don't you believe me? Tell me why I would instigate divorce proceedings if I were in love with my wife? And give me one good reason why I should lie to you?'

'I can't.' Nor could she. 'But you can stop looking daggers at me, I'm not going to apologise. If I made a mistake, I made a mistake.'

He looked heavenwards. 'You can say that again!' He threw down the rest of his drink. 'All right. Then that's that little matter cleared up. Come on, let's see what's in the refrigerator. Lunch is going to be a joint effort, Miss Rebecca Hill.'

Trouble loomed during the last week of November. Becky had not been to Stirling's apartment again. She hadn't been asked to. Nor had he attempted to kiss her, not even in the most perfunctory way. He had done no more than hold her hand. In fact she was beginning to feel foolish. She was also, in honesty, extremely chagrined, not to mention frustrated, because he had resisted her for so long.

All in all, she had a problem.

It would not be true to say it had been easy for Stirling, she knew that well enough; she could read his desire in his eyes, but he had behaved like a too-perfect gentleman and she was wishing now that he wouldn't. Not to this extent. There were times when his very nearness, the touch of his hand alone, was enough to arouse her. This was something she would never have believed possible, that she could feel this way, given that she had never actually known what it was to be physically fulfilled by a man.

Loving him only added to her difficulty. Sometimes she would look at him and feel as if her heart were bursting, and in being unable to express it she felt as if there were a dam inside her. But she couldn't express her love, not even with words, especially not with words. For weeks he had been there for her, behaving like a friend, taking her to the theatre, the ballet, the opera, to restaurants and clubs and casinos, talking with her, walking with her—anything she wanted. He had been selfless and giving, charming, attentive, entertaining. The perfect companion. But he had never told her how he really felt about her. Nor did he ever speak about the future—no further than tomorrow.

No further than tomorrow. She, too, did not dare to think further than that. Loving Stirling Robard had added a new dimension to her life; one that she could not regret, no matter what happened. When this relationship ended it would be painful in the extreme, but for the moment, at least, she could not envisage ever regretting it.

She glanced at him surreptitiously now, as she got into his Mercedes, wondering what was on his mind. He had been very subdued all evening, which was most unusual, and she sensed that things were coming to a head.

'What's wrong, Stirling?' She spoke quietly in the confines of the car when he made no effort to switch the engine on. They were parked in the West End, the noise of passers-by going unnoticed by them both.

'Rebecca, would there be any point in my asking you back to my apartment? I mean——'

'I know what you mean.'

'No, you don't. I just thought it would be nice to eat in for a change. That's all I'm asking of you.'

The idea of that was blissful, so much so that she wanted to laugh. Her home was always full of people: friends, friends of friends. It was invariably noisy and often downright chaotic. And, quite apart from that, she was sick and tired of eating out.

'But,' he added, softly but pointedly. 'I can't guarantee to keep my hands off you. I'm—not sure how much more I can take.'

A faint drizzle had started. Becky looked at the windscreen and at the dazzle of the West End's lights beyond it, thinking. He had warned her and she wanted to say yes, she wanted to be alone with him, to be in his arms...to be one with him.

But what would that cost her? How high the price? Would it be the beginning of the end? Did he really care for her or had he merely been biding his time? Stirling was not a man easily daunted, she knew that from experience; he got what he wanted and he wanted her—physically. She did not underestimate, and never had underestimated, either his cleverness or his determination.

'Rebecca? For heaven's sake, say something!'

'All right, let's go.' She turned to face him, deciding to take her chances. 'We'll go to your place.'

By the time they got to his apartment in Knightsbridge, they were laughing. They had stopped off at a take-away, a simple every-day occurrence that was for them a treat. While Stirling was in the bathroom, she was putting the food on to plates.

They ate in the living-room, their plates on low coffee-tables to begin with, on their knees moments later. They were laughing again, talking about roughing it and what a nice change it was.

'There was a time when I thought I'd never get sick of eating in fancy restaurants,' she told him, 'and I never thought I'd get bored with parties and——'

'And have you?' he asked, seeming surprised. 'Got bored with parties, I mean?'

'Definitely. Long since. Haven't you?'

'Long since,' he agreed. 'But I had assumed you still enjoyed that kind of life. Don't tell me I've been boring you, taking you out and about every night?'

His concern, genuine as it obviously was, created a constriction around her heart. For seconds it was difficult to breathe.

'OK,' he went on jovially. 'You won't tell me. Because you wouldn't be so unkind, would you?' He put his plate down with a contented sigh. 'It's not in your nature.'

'I wouldn't tell you,' she said, finishing her own last mouthful, 'because it wouldn't be true. There's no way I could be bored with you, Stirling. You're too...' She stopped, having heard clearly the tenderness in her voice, realising just in time that she had been in danger of wearing her heart on her sleeve.

'Too what?'

She bit her lip, cursing herself, dissembling, successfully, by laughing again. 'Too what is right, my friend!'

But he wasn't laughing. 'Too what, my darling? Too much?'

She answered without looking at him. 'No.'

'Too little.'

'Never.'

'Then what?'

The ensuing silence screamed at her. From the street several storeys below came the sound of traffic, muffled in reality, suddenly inaudible to Becky. Reality. Was this really reality? Oddly, she felt as if she might be nothing more than a character in someone else's dream. She didn't feel normal, didn't feel like herself. She was experiencing again that awful rushing sound in her ears, she could hear nothing but that and the beating of her own heart. She was aware of nothing but the nearness of Stirling, sitting just two feet away from her on the settee. Him, and his aura of expectation; he was waiting for an answer and she hadn't the faintest idea what she could say without . . . without letting him know that she loved him . . . hopelessly.

'Rebecca?'

'I'll make some coffee——'

'No. Don't move, please.' He shook his head as if to clear it, he was looking intently at her and it was all she could do to withstand the searching of his eyes. 'You never cease to surprise me, do you know that? Even before I followed you to London, I—well, I'd had to revise my understanding of you several times. Whenever I'd thought I knew you, you behaved in ways that proved me wrong. It's still happening, I'm still discovering what and who you really are . . . and I have to say it's a pleasurable process. I want to know everything about you, I want to know all there is to know. I want——'

'Stirling, please don't go on. I know what you want, I'm neither blind nor stupid.'

His smile was gentle, the inclination of his head speaking volumes. 'All right, certainly I want that—you. I won't deny how I long to discover you . . . in every way. I want to explore you physically, naturally I do; I want to touch you, to kiss you, to know every inch of——'

'Stop it, please.' It was a quiet protest but it was a protest. She couldn't handle this, his talking like this, his looking at her like this.

'I can't,' he said, equally quietly, 'I've suppressed too much for too long. Rebecca . . .' And then he moved, just the short distance he needed to in order to touch her. It took only a second for his arms to come around her, and that was the beginning of the end.

With an involuntary cry she leaned against him, moving willingly into his reaching arms, revelling in the feel of them, in the warmth of him, the very scent of him. She had waited so long for this, too long. She had dreamt about how it would be to feel once again the warm, firm pressure of his mouth on hers. And now it was happening.

How long it lasted, she never knew, exactly. From some unsuspected depth in her, unsuspected even by herself, alien to herself, there came another cry, one that she could hear but Stirling perhaps could not. It was a sound that emanated from beyond her physical needs, it was something that struck at, or came from, the very essence of her being. She heard it in her temples, in her ears, in her heart—but she did not know whether it had got as far as her mouth.

What she did know, and it was really all she understood for the moment, was that she was holding Stirling at arm's length. He was uncharacteristically cursing—and she was half naked. The dress she was wearing was off her shoulders, its top peeled down almost to her waist, and her bra was undone. It was as if there had been a time-lag, a suspension in her consciousness, until the moment when Stirling's lips had covered the erect peak of her breast...

'For heaven's sake, Rebecca! What's *wrong*?'

'I—I'm...' She closed her eyes against the look on his face, wishing she could blot out the ragged sound of his breathing. He had seen his hands trembling but it was worse than that, his arousal was such that all of him was shaking, she could feel it even though he was no longer touching her. 'I'm sorry,' she finished lamely. She fastened her bra and pulled her dress back into place, flinching at the sound of pure frustration he emitted.

He wrenched away from her furiously, pushing himself to his feet to pace around the room. When finally he

could speak, he said, 'That's *not* what I want to hear!
I don't want an apology, I want an explanation.'

She forced herself to meet his eyes. 'I just . . . can't go
through with it.'

'Damn it, I've realised that! What I want to know is
why? Why not?'

She looked away because she was about to lie, there
was nothing else she could do. How could she tell him
of her fear of being thought easy, her fear of being
likened to the woman he was divorcing? To tell him that
would be to tell him how very much she cared. 'I don't
know.'

He closed his eyes, visibly struggling for composure.
'I swear I'll never understand you! Like hell you don't
know!'

Wishing herself elsewhere was pointless, wishing
herself invisible was pointless. She could feel his anger
and his frustration across the space separating them, they
were almost tangible. 'I think you'd better take me home,
Stirling. Or would you rather I take a taxi?'

He almost exploded then. Becky saw his eyes flash
dangerously, brilliantly and darkly, but that lasted for
only a second. It was immediately replaced by something resembling pain—and that look did not disappear.
'You're not going anywhere,' he said hoarsely. 'Not until
you tell me what you want.'

'What—I don't know what you mean.'

At that, Stirling lost his battle for composure. He
roared at her. 'You don't know? Will you stop *saying*
that!'

Becky didn't answer; she let silence hang in the air
because she was afraid to trigger him further. She simply
didn't know how to appease him. She glanced helplessly
around the room, thinking about the dire mistake she

had made in coming here again; she had been asking for trouble and she'd got it.

Stirling had turned his back to her. He was standing with his head bowed, with both hands flat against the wall, leaving Becky in no doubt that he felt like strangling her, that he had moved about as far away as he could get because he could no longer trust himself to be near her. 'Look,' he said at length, 'supposing you just tell me. It can't be that difficult. Be straight with me, tell me where this relationship is heading—because one thing's for sure, I can't go on with things as they are.'

'Then let's end it right now!' she blurted angrily.

He turned, looking stunned, staring at her if he'd never seen her before. 'End it ...?'

Becky stood up. She had to get out of here. He wasn't the only one who couldn't go on like this. He had no idea that it was even more difficult for her, that on top of everything else she had the awful uncertainty to contend with. Uncertainty? No, it was just the opposite. She had the certain knowledge, she had always had, that this relationship was going precisely nowhere. Furthermore, it was high time she told him that. 'I'll tell you where this relationship is heading—to its inevitable conclusion. And this is it. It's over, Stirling!' She snatched up her coat from the nearby armchair, her coat and her handbag.

'Wait a minute!' He was at her side in a flash, dropping both hands heavily on to her shoulders. 'Rebecca, that's no answer. What's so awful about the prospect of going to bed with me? Why do I get the impression you resent me for wanting you? *What* is so awful about that? What the hell do you think I'm made of?'

'I don't resent you for it. I want you, too, remember.'

'Then why behave the way you do? Why deny us both the pleasure?'

She sighed, resignedly, hopelessly. 'Stirling, it isn't that simple, not for me.' He was looking deeply into her eyes, waiting for her to say more, but she couldn't.

'Go on,' he urged, and, when she shook her head, 'Darling, please! Tell me what you're thinking, talk to me. We have to sort this out, I can't stand——' To her astonishment his voice cracked. Briefly he glanced away before bringing his eyes back to hers. 'Rebecca, I think I'm in love with you...'

It took seconds before she could respond, seconds which she needed before she could trust herself to speak. On hearing those words she had allowed herself to hope, it had flared inside her like a fiery torch, only to be doused because she knew he was mistaken—or, worse, that he might simply be saying the obvious in order to get what he wanted, what she had admitted to wanting herself.

'No,' she managed at last. 'If you think you're in love with me, you should think again. Remember that you've made that mistake once before——'

'I don't need reminding of that.' He caught hold of her chin, preventing her from looking elsewhere. 'And that's the problem, isn't it? You think all my feelings for you reside in the area below my belt.'

'Stirling——'

'I *have* to say what I'm thinking,' he told her. 'Well, you're wrong if that is what you think. For heaven's sake, we've spent so much time together, surely you can't imagine that you're no more than a sex object to me?'

'No,' she said honestly. She didn't think that; she knew how much he enjoyed her company, her sense of humour, the long talks they had. She knew also that she never had been simply a sex object to him. 'But I am a challenge to you.'

His smile was rueful. 'There was—no, there still is, an element of truth in that. But there's more to my wanting you than that, much more. I have no problem with my ego, if that's what you mean, I don't perceive myself to be diminished by your rejection. I can take no for an answer, I've demonstrated that. Witness tonight; when you called a halt I didn't try to persuade you. You see,' he added softly, 'I don't want to do anything that you don't want, too. With your mind, not just with your body.' He let go of her, as if he had given up on her. 'There's no way I'll even try to take advantage of you, to take you against your will. Tonight I—well, I wasn't misreading the signals you gave me.'

No, he hadn't misread them, she had moved very willingly into his arms, she had come to his apartment knowing full well what would happen. Some of it, at least.

In the face of her silence, he added, 'Rebecca, you don't want to finish with me any more than I want to finish with you. Will you admit that much?'

'Yes.' It was no more than a whisper. 'But it won't last, Stirling.'

He caught hold of her again, shaking her this time. 'Why? Why not? Do you say that because I'm married? That won't be for much longer——'

'I know.'

'Then *why*?' he persisted. But he didn't give her a chance to answer—for which she was very grateful. His brow cleared suddenly, as if he had been inspired. 'Listen, let me show you I'm serious, let's put our relationship on to a proper footing, a realistic one. Move in with me.'

CHAPTER ELEVEN

CALMLY, Becky stepped aside to put on her coat. Automatically Stirling reached for it, helping her into it, and she was glad to have her back to him if only for a moment or two.

She did not need even to consider his suggestion, it was out of the question. Moving in with him was no answer, either. For her it would only postpone the inevitable ending. There was no denying she had hoped for more than the suggestion that she live with him, just as there was no denying the fact that marriage had clearly lost all its appeal to him.

'Rebecca?' He put his arms around her when she turned to face him, holding her loosely within their circle. 'You've mentioned that you'd like to get out of that house anyway, if only for some peace. So why not move in with me?'

She smiled what she hoped was a neutral sort of smile. 'Sorry, that doesn't appeal to me in the least.'

He smiled, too, his arms closing more tightly. He pulled her against him, putting his lips to her temple and laughing softly. 'I don't believe that. I'm not blind, either—I happen to be confident that your feelings for me go further than this.' The movement of his hand, the sudden touch of it against her breast, sent a jolt of shock into the pit of her stomach.

'Stirling——'

'Don't worry,' he said, moving his hand away, around to her back. It was inside her open coat, though, and the feel of it nestling there was nearly as sensual as it had been a moment ago. 'That was just a little joke, Rebecca.' He let go of her altogether then, except for the retaining hand on her shoulder. 'Tell me you'll think about it,' he insisted. 'And then I'll take you home.'

If that was the only way she was going to get out of here, she thought, then she would have to do just that. She told him what he wanted to hear, and if he noticed that her voice was flat, totally without conviction, he didn't show it. 'I'll think about it,' she lied, and watched him smile, nodding in satisfaction.

It was very late when they pulled up outside her home. Stirling brought the car to a halt and glanced at the windows. 'Looks as if there's a party going on.'

'Do you want to come in?'

'Frankly, no.'

Becky couldn't help laughing. 'Can't say I blame you.' Stupidly, quite without thinking, she added, 'Oh, to live in peace and quiet!' As soon as the words were out, she regretted them.

'The offer has been made,' Stirling said. He leaned towards her and cut the engine. 'We could have a beautiful life together, you know. We could live quietly in Lucerne, or here in London if you found Switzerland began to pall. And there again, if you missed an element of chaos in your life, we could spend some time in New York.' In the light of the streetlamp she saw the flash of his teeth as he smiled, the charming, cajoling nature of it almost making her heart stop. 'Anything you like, Rebecca. It could be very good indeed, there'd be no need for you to work if you didn't want to. But if you did,' he added quickly, 'that would be fine by me.' He reached for her, but what he said next served only as an unnecessary reminder that a commitment was no part of his thinking. 'It would last as long as it lasted and it would be a hell of a lot of fun.' With that, he pulled her into his arms. 'Do you know that you're driving me slowly out of my mind?'

'I know you're being dramatic,' she countered, flirting quite deliberately. It was difficult to part from him in spite of everything—as soon as they had left his apartment her desire to get away from him had ceased, no doubt because she no longer felt in danger. 'Now go home, Stirling. I have to be up early and I'm not going to get my full quota of sleep as it is.'

He appeared not to hear her, his mouth closed over hers and within seconds a hand was straying to cover her breast again. But that was as far as it went. He raised his head, letting his thumb move in a lazy circle over the tip of her breast, just for a second or two. 'I'm going. But I'll be very lucky if I sleep at all...'

It was the same with Becky. She let herself into the house unheard, unnoticed, bypassed the living-room and went straight to her bedroom. It was time to move out, in fact it was long overdue. She could easily afford to rent a place of her own, she could even buy a house if she wanted to; there would be no problem in getting a mortgage.

Hitherto it had not been important enough to do anything about and in earlier days, much earlier days, it had been fun sharing with three other models. But times had changed. She had changed. Her priorities were very different nowadays; what once had made her happy now left her cold. She really did want peace and quiet, she really did not want the hectic life she had lived. Tears came to her eyes when she thought of what she really wanted. She wanted to be married to Stirling, she wanted to have his children and she wanted . . . but none of that had been included in the picture he had painted just now.

'Becky? This is very anti-social of you!' Ingrid burst into the room, a little drunk, laughing giddily. 'I saw the car and—what's the matter?'

'Sorry, I couldn't even face saying goodnight to them.' Rebecca nodded in the direction of the living-room. 'Is it going to go on all night?'

'Who knows?'

'I have to be up early in the morning, I'll be lucky if I can sleep through that lot.'

'It's never stopped you before.'

Ingrid was wrong about that but Becky didn't bother putting her right. 'I don't know why we've never been evicted from this house.'

'Of course you know why, it's because we always invite the neighbours in—best way of preventing 'em from complaining to the landlord!'

Becky's smile was thin, born on a sigh. 'I suppose so.'

Ingrid came closer, peering carefully at her. 'Do you want to talk?'

There was only the slightest hesitation. 'I—Stirling asked me to move in with him.'

'He did?' Ingrid was delighted. 'Well, that's great! So his heart *is* in the right place——'

'What do you mean by that?'

'Isn't it obvious? It means he's serious, far more than we'd thought——'

'No!' Becky almost shouted the word. 'You're not a stupid girl, Ingrid—just think about it, will you? Take two seconds to think about it! What do you suppose his motives are?'

The other girl's mouth had fallen open at Becky's outburst. It was out of character and it had come as a shock—it was also very informative. 'I think your re-action tells me all I need to know,' she said. 'You're in way over your head, aren't you? It's even worse than I thought...you do want marriage, don't you? The whole bit?'

Very quietly, Becky admitted it. Admitted it? Was it something to be ashamed of? 'People change, Ingrid. There was a time when I thought of marriage as being— but never mind that. Yes, it is what I want. Now. With Stirling.'

'So what did you say to his offer?'

'I said no.'

'And his reaction?'

'He asked me to think about it. I said I would but I don't need to, I only said that in order to get out of his apartment.'

Ingrid's eyebrows shot up. 'His apartment? But I thought——'

'I know. And no, before you ask, it didn't happen.'

Ingrid sat down, shaking her head, totally unable to understand.

'Don't say it,' Becky warned. 'Because you're not the only one who doesn't understand me. Stirling doesn't either. Sometimes I don't understand me myself.'

Ingrid didn't say it, she just looked at Becky with sympathy. 'I hate to see you hurting like this. I'll—go back to the party then. You going to be out all day tomorrow?'

'Till about four, provided nothing goes wrong.' She had a photographic session in the morning, and heaven alone knew what she was going to look like. She felt exhausted both physically and mentally.

It took all her skill with make-up to get herself looking right the next morning. Age was still on her side, of course, but the day would come when liberties like the one she had taken last night would not be so easy to hide. It was a sobering thought, one that kept popping into her head all day. Maybe she should quit modelling now, start looking for shop premises...

But her enthusiasm had gone. There was only one future that appealed to her.

It was five-thirty when she got home and the house was empty, wonderfully, quietly empty. Becky headed straight for the kitchen and the kettle, wondering whether Stirling had called. If he had, there would be a note by the kettle—provided he had caught someone at home, of course.

He had, and there was a note. It had been written by Patti, who had been very conscientious about passing on messages since her telling off, and it was marked nine thirty-five a.m. It read, 'Stirling just rang and I'm on my way out so I must be brief. He said he'd been called away, he's got to go to the States, but he'll ring you from there as soon as poss. 'Bye. Patti. PS Neither Janice nor I will be home tonight.'

Rebecca sank on to a kitchen chair. Stirling had been called away? What did this mean? What did it really mean? Had he been called away on business? Presumably. It must be an emergency, something that required the presence of the big boss.

Or maybe it was Angel. Maybe he was responding to yet another plea for help. No. Angel was in a villa in Spain, wasn't she? Or had she returned to America?

Anything could have happened, it could be anything.

She made the tea she had been gasping for and told herself not to worry. It proved to be easier in the thinking than in the doing, though, and she caught herself calculating how long it would take him to get to America, to get to a telephone. If he had flown to the East Coast, to New York . . . Impatiently, she drained her cup and went upstairs to take a bath, telling herself she was at least guaranteed an early night tonight. It would be strange, not seeing Stirling. It already felt strange.

His telephone call did not come. Twenty-four hours later Becky was sitting at the kitchen table again, drinking tea and still worrying. The sound of a key in the door brought her quickly to her feet, hoping it was Patti.

It was. She almost collided with Becky as she came into the kitchen. 'Hello, Legs. Is there any tea in that pot?'

'Yes, help yourself. Listen, Patti, I haven't heard a word from Stirling——'

'I thought you looked down in the mouth. Missing him, are you? Can't say I blame you, I'd miss him too, if he were mine. But why should I beat about the bush?' she went on, laughing at herself. 'I think Stirling Robard is something else, and if you ever tire of him . . .'

The easiest thing was to laugh with her, and to say, yes, she was missing him, and to let Patti think whatever she liked. Both she and Janice would be taking it for granted that Stirling was Becky's lover; they both knew she always came home at night, and that she always had since they'd lived with her, but they no doubt assumed that her love life was merely managed differently from theirs. It was only Ingrid who knew how things really were with Becky, only Ingrid who knew the real state of affairs. Or rather, she thought humourlessly, the lack of them. 'Patti, tell me what he said when he rang, would you? Your note told me nothing.'

There was a frown, a shrug. 'I'm sorry, Becky, there's nothing I can add, really. He sounded distracted, obviously in a hurry and eager to get off the phone as fast as he could. Yes, come to think of it must have been in a hurry, he did mention that he was flying on Concorde...'

'To where?'

'He didn't say. But that would be New York, wouldn't it?'

'So it was business? He's been called away on business?'

Patti seemed surprised. 'Well, I'd taken that much for granted. Why else might he be called away?' she went on, becoming intrigued.

'I can't imagine. Not to worry,' she added lightly. 'He'll ring when he rings.'

It was three o'clock in the morning when he did finally call. Becky heard the trill of the phone and flung herself out of bed to answer it before it disturbed anyone else. She had been a long way from sleep, and for once the other three girls had all gone to bed before midnight that night.

'Rebecca?'

It was a bad line but she could tell immediately that something was very wrong, even from that one word. 'Stirling! Where are you?'

'I'm in...'

'What? Where?' She couldn't catch the word, it was either the fault of her ears, the line, or it was the very unlikelihood of it, but she thought he said he was in Florida.

'I'm in Florida.'

'But why?' Unconsciously her hand tightened on the receiver. He didn't have offices in Florida, it had to be... 'Is it something to do with Angel?'

'Yes. She——'

'Did she contact you? Is she——?' For just a second she hesitated, fearing the answer she might get. *All* her fears were resurrecting themselves now, the fear that she had been wrong to believe he didn't love his wife, the fear that he had been mistaken in believing that, the fear that Angel might love him, the fear that she had reacted to the divorce proceedings by trying to get him back.

Fear.

She wanted to be sick. Her heart was thumping crazily in her chest, that awful rushing noise was in her ears again and it made it impossible to hear what he had just said. At least, she thought he'd just said something. 'Stirling? I—is it about the divorce? Is that why she got in touch with you?'

There followed a silence. It had nothing to do with the telephone line, which was clearing itself by the second. He was, Becky knew, being silent because he didn't know how to answer her. With her heart in her mouth she waited, unable to prompt him any more.

At last he spoke. His voice came over strongly and clearly, so much so that there was no room for error this time. 'There isn't going to be a divorce...'

Rebecca's eyes closed. She felt faint. The room shifted on its axis and her mind screamed at her. She should have known, she should have known...

'Rebecca? Did you hear what I just told you? She's dead, Rebecca. Angel is dead.'

CHAPTER TWELVE

BECKY was waiting for him in Heathrow Airport, scanning faces as the first trickle of people emerged from Customs. Stirling was among the first. She noticed immediately that he had no luggage, that he was carrying only a briefcase, and her heart flipped over painfully at the sight of him.

'Stirling!' She waved, moving quickly towards him as he held out his free hand, clasping hers possessively. He looked tired, strained. She knew he'd had a bad time, whatever his feelings for Angel had been or had not been. His wife had been killed in a yachting accident off the Florida coast, one of those freak accidents that should never have happened, and there had been an inquiry, an inquest which Stirling had attended.

And, of course, there had been the funeral.

It seemed as if an eternity had passed since she had seen him; in fact it was less than two weeks but they had been bad days for her, days of anxiety and speculation. It hadn't been possible to have a sensible conversation with him over the phone, over such a distance and in all the circumstances. In any event she'd been afraid to ask too much in case she heard something she didn't want to hear.

They collected his Mercedes from the car park, where he had left it on his way out of the country, and he drove straight to his apartment without asking whether she wanted to go there with him; there was nowhere else to go to be private. He said little on the journey and nothing of any importance. He remarked on the weather, on the rain that was belting against the windscreen. In less than two weeks Christmas would be upon them and there was already the threat, or the promise, of snow, if the weathermen were to be believed.

Stirling poured himself a Scotch the moment they got indoors, a very stiff one, she noticed.

'Hey,' he said, watching her watching him. 'Take that worried look off your face, will you? I'm not about to get plastered, if that's what you're thinking. I've seen enough of that to last me a lifetime. So take it easy; I'm fine, apart from being tired and stiff and unwashed.' He took a sip from his glass and smiled vaguely. 'You'll discover in time that one reaches a stage in life when there is nothing one can't handle. I've reached that stage, anyway, and I don't mean just recently. It wasn't a pleasant scenario in the States but it was manageable.'

She accepted the glass of red wine he had poured for her and watched him throw down the rest of his Scotch—neat. 'I'm not worried about you, Stirling. You're a big boy, all grown up and more than capable.' She doubted she would ever reach the stage he had just described, most certainly not in the next twelve years anyway, by which time she would be as old as he was now. There again, she was in no doubt that he'd crammed a lot more living into his years than she had—he had certainly had a lot of experiences she hadn't had.

'I was thinking about your father,' she said, 'and how things were for you when you were young.'

'Younger,' he corrected, grinning.

'Younger, of course I meant that! No, seriously, I wanted to tell you that your father, well, that it was a factor I had—not thought about carefully enough. I mean, in relation to Angel...'

He nodded. 'You're right. My experience with my father, watching him destroy himself, was very much an influence on me as far as Angel was concerned. I'd been unable to help him, unable even to stand it, to witness it, which is why I used to come to your home during the holidays. But I was younger then. I was young, as you said, full stop.' He sighed, shrugging, his voice nothing more and nothing less than philosophical as he went on, 'When Angel ran into trouble it was different, I was different, I thought I might be able to help—albeit from a distance. I tried, anyway. When I finally got her into that clinic, I was hopeful for her but not entirely. Experience had taught me that people who are hooked on drink fall back on their dependency as often as not. Especially when they're as unhappy or lonely as Dad was, as Angel was...'

He ran his hands through his hair. He was still standing by the drinks cabinet, clearly not sufficiently at ease to sit down. 'But it's all over now...'

There was a silence. Becky broke it. 'What was she doing in Florida?'

'She'd gone there with her boyfriend, the bloke whose villa she'd been staying at in Puerto Banus. He kept a yacht there, as well as one in Florida, and they all drowned, the crew as well as the merrymakers. They'd been hopping around—hell, never mind all that. Suffice it to say that Angel is out of it now.'

Becky closed her eyes. Out of it. Yes, she was, poor girl.

The sound of Stirling's voice brought her eyes open. He was telling her again to take it easy, sensing what she was thinking. She looked at him and found him smiling; it was a smile so warm and appreciative that it melted all her anxieties, making her confident enough not to mind when he asked if she would excuse him for fifteen minutes. 'I want to shower and shave, then I'll be more human. Would you mind, Rebecca?'

'Not at all. I know the feeling.'

'Really? Since when have you felt the need for a shave?' He walked past her, ruffling her hair and laughing as if he were the happiest man on earth. Was it an act? Bravado? He seemed so—so *normal*.

When he rejoined her it was exactly fifteen minutes later and he had changed into black trousers and a thick, creamy-coloured polo neck sweater. In the short time he'd been gone, twilight had turned into darkness and Becky had closed the curtains. She'd kicked off her shoes and was curled up on the settee now, her legs tucked under her. Stirling switched on lamps and turned off the main light, going over to switch on the electric fire in the marble fireplace that was a feature of the room. The flat was centrally heated and plenty warm enough but he obviously didn't think so. She watched him as he bent, her eyes shifting to the artificial flames of the fire when they leapt into action.

'If we were at my home in Switzerland,' he said softly, turning to look at her, 'I'd make a real fire, a log fire. Now wouldn't that be cosy?'

'Very.' Her response came quietly; she guessed what he was about to say next and she knew exactly what she would say.

The question didn't come. She wondered whether he had gone off the idea of her living with him.

She wondered about a lot of things.

'Rebecca...?'

'Mm?'

'Are you hungry?'

She laughed because she had been expecting such a different question, the other question. 'No. Are you?'

'No.'

'Just as well, there probably isn't a scrap of food in the place.'

He refilled his glass, this time adding a generous measure of soda to his Scotch. She held out her glass and he poured more wine for her, putting both glasses on the low table in front of the settee before he sat down next to her. 'There might be an egg or two in the fridge. There might even be half a dozen.'

'Good grief!' she laughed, looking heavenwards. 'You just don't know what you're worth, do you?'

'You're right,' he said, laughing with her. 'Because for all I know, there might be a dozen!'

'Who looks after you here—anyone?'

'There's a lady who comes in when the place needs cleaning. I leave that to the porter to arrange. She would come in daily if it were necessary.'

'But you don't make much mess?'

'I do little more than sleep here, as you know very well. I—this isn't a home, Rebecca. More's the pity...' And still he didn't ask her whether she had thought about his offer. Well, she wasn't going to volunteer an answer.

Only then did she become aware of the tension in him, in the attitude of his body, the way he picked up his glass, the tone of his voice, as if he were trying too hard, now, to be his usual self. 'I missed you something awful.'

'I missed you, too.' She twisted around in order to look at him, unaware of her skirt riding up a little as she did so. She was leaning into the corner of the settee and he was only inches away from her—which was where he stayed. His eyes shifted to her legs, to the exposure of her lower thighs.

'I'd appreciate it if you'd do something about that,' he said, moving his gaze from her legs to her face. 'Keeping my hands off you is difficult enough as it is, without being obviously reminded of your charms.'

Hastily she yanked her skirt down, flushing slightly. 'Sorry.'

'I feared you would be,' he said, but there was a smile in his voice. 'I'll say this for you, you really don't tease consciously. It just comes naturally.'

'Stirling——'

'You see? You're still too much to resist.' He put his hand on her foot, his fingers curling around it and moving rhythmically, as if it had been made for caressing. It was extremely pleasant and it became more so, of which he was no doubt fully aware. Within seconds desire was stirring in her; this, without so much as a kiss or...but who was she trying to kid? He had only to look at her to make her want him. 'So tell me, Rebecca, because I need to know, has anything changed?'

'I'm—not sure what you mean.'

'Yes you are. I mean I want to make love to you. Now. Right here and now. I want to make love to you all night long, I want to kiss you but, if I do, I won't be able to stop, I'll want to go on kissing you and tasting you, all of you, every inch of you——'

She almost recoiled. His words were arousing her further and to her disgust she was blushing furiously, feeling gauche and unsophisticated. His ensuing laughter made it obvious that he knew what her answer would be, that he knew nothing had changed.

'You're unreal,' he told her. 'Do you know that? I think I must be dreaming all this, I've never met a woman who——' He broke off, looking at her with a sudden, quick flash of realisation. 'Tell me something...what does this monumental self-control of yours spring from? Have you been badly hurt or something? I mean any kind of hurt—emotional or—physical.' He said the last word as if he hoped it were not the case, the look in his eyes a mixture of anger and distaste, and concern. 'Is that it, darling? Have you——'

'No,' she whispered. 'No, no, nothing like that.'

'Then how do you manage——'

'I've told you before, my head rules.'

And then it came. 'Then tell me, what did your head make of my suggestion that we live together?'

'It told me it was a lousy idea.'

Her answer surprised him, she was aware of that. 'Why?'

She looked away, feeling as if her heart would crack in two from the pain it was in—it was still trying desperately to have the final say. 'Because it's not what it—what I—want.'

The ensuing silence seemed endless, it stretched on and on and on, until she felt she would scream if it didn't stop.

'Then I don't know what else I can say.' Stirling moved his hand from her foot, a withdrawal in more ways than one.

Neither did she, so she didn't even try. She was trembling inside, her hands were visibly trembling and she crossed her arms across her chest, tucking her hands out of sight.

Stirling shifted too, he picked up his glass and drained it, slowly shaking his head. 'I told you, I can't go on like this—with the status quo.' He glanced at her, briefly, as if he couldn't bear to look at her fully. 'If you're not prepared to——

'What?' It sounded as if an ultimatum were on the horizon and it angered her. 'What, Stirling? Spit it out.'

'If you're not prepared to change things, then maybe you were right in saying we should end it . . .'

Which was fine by her! At least, that was how it felt right then, in her anger, before there was time for it to sink in fully. 'Fine. That's fine by me, Stirling!' She uncoiled herself and reached for her shoes, shrugging away the hand that dropped on her shoulder.

'Rebecca——'

'No! Rebecca nothing. If I'm not prepared to jump into bed with you, it's over, that's what you're saying and that's——'

'Jump? *Jump?* For pity's sake! Just how long would it take? That's what I'd like to know!'

'As long as I wanted it to. As long as *I* wanted it to, have you got that?' She was on her feet, shoving them into her shoes and looking around for her bag.

He made no effort to stop her this time, he just stayed where he was, seated, looking at her as if he thought she would change her mind. 'You're being totally unreasonable——'

'Go to hell!' She snatched up her bag and walked swiftly from the room, collecting her coat from the hall as she left, pulling the outer door closed with a bang.

He didn't pursue her, nor did she wait for the lift, just in case he came after her. She took the stairs down to the street and wondered how long it would be before she found a taxi in this weather for it was still pouring with rain.

CHAPTER THIRTEEN

'BRACE yourself,' Ingrid said. 'You're in for a surprise. Or rather a shock.' She held up her hand, as if to prevent Becky from moving any further along the hallway. At the sound of the key in the door she had fled to meet her—and Becky's face had spoken volumes as soon as she looked at her.

'What is it? Come on, Ingrid, you can see I'm in no mood for jokes right now!' She had been halfway home before she had found a taxi, half running, half walking, unseeing, unable to take in what had happened. From the living-room came the sound of voices, several of them—she might have known there would be no peace when she got home, no way she could be alone tonight.

'You look like a drowned rat. Where's Stirling? What's happened?'

'Not now, Ingrid. It's off. Finished. Finito. I was presented with an ultimatum: "If I can't have your body, I don't want to know you."'

'Bloody hell! Is that what he said?'

'Not exactly, but that's what it amounted to. Don't look so shocked, I'm not.'

'But—what about the rest of it? Angel? How he felt about her? Were you right, after all, in thinking he might still be in love with her?'

'No. He never was, no more than he's in love with me, either. And that's enough, Ingrid. I told you, I don't want to discuss it now, all I want to do is get to bed.'

'I'm—afraid you can't do that, Becky. Not just yet.' She glanced over her shoulder at the door to the living-room. 'Michael McCaffrey is sitting in there, with two of his entourage. Patti and Janice are entertaining them—as you can hear.' There was a burst of laughter, the sound of male and female voices mingling.

Dumbstruck, Rebecca could do no more than repeat the name. 'Michael McCaffrey? *Michael McCaffrey?*'

'None other. He just turned up, about an hour ago. He said he got in from the States this afternoon, he didn't say why—except that he was missing you.'

'Oh, no! I don't believe this——' It was too much, it was bizarre. He'd got in from the States this afternoon? He might even have been on the same flight as Stirling; Stirling had come from Florida via New York...

'Believe it.' Ingrid wasn't smiling; this was no joke. 'He really is the crazy artist, isn't he? Fun, though, as you said. You should see what he's wearing!'

Rebecca had no interest at all in what Michael McCaffrey was wearing—all she wanted to do was to get rid of him, get him off the premises as quickly as possible.

It wasn't that easy, it wasn't easy at all. She marched into the living-room, not pausing to think that she must look like an irate bailiff or something—a very wet one at that. 'Michael? Well, I must say——'

'Surprise, surprise!' For a big man he shot to his feet with amazing speed, crossing over to her and raising her hand to his lips. Stupidly she let him, blinking at his effusiveness, at his very presence in her living-room. 'I've missed you, honey. I missed you from the moment you left New York, so I thought I'd come and see you, give my eyes a treat. Well, say something! Aren't you pleased to see me?'

Everyone was looking at her expectantly. She nodded to his friends, both of whom she knew, and caught the glint of amusement in the eyes of Patti and Janice. Ingrid was still in the doorway, standing behind her like a sentry.

'Delighted. Of course I'm pleased to see you. But I'm——' It was all she had time for, a polite response to which she had been going to add the explanation that she was extremely sorry but he would really have to ring her tomorrow because she was so tired right now . . . But there wasn't time for that because the telephone was ringing in the hall. Ingrid was the nearest to it, and she was already on her way to it.

Her, 'Stirling! How are you?' was all too audible to Becky—and to the other girls. Then there was a pause and Ingrid's hesitant, 'Yes, she's just got in, actually.'

'Excuse me.' Rebecca stepped back into the hall, closing the living-room door behind her. 'Why did you say that?' she accused Ingrid, who had her hand over the mouthpiece.

'What else could I say? If I'd said you weren't in yet he'd have been suspicious, or frantic. You can't avoid him, Becky, it's pointless. If you don't talk to him now, he'll only ring again. Come on, get it over with.'

This time she really had to brace herself. Michael McCaffrey's appearance was nothing compared to this trauma. She took the telephone from Ingrid and asked Stirling point-blank what he wanted.

'I wanted to know you were home safely.' His voice was all wrong, unlike anything she had heard before.

'Well, I am. And you're as drunk as a lord.'

'A little, a little. Well, perhaps more than a little,' he admitted. 'And I can't blame me, can you?' he asked unsteadily. 'There's a first time for everything, they tell me. Speaking of which, another thought has occurred to me. Are you a virgin, Rebecca? Is that why you're so hung up about going to bed with me? Am I being too ridiculous or could there be something in this? Is it possible——?'

Anything was possible! 'Speaking of which,' she cut in, her voice dripping irony, '*you're* the one who's hung up!' And he was. She had slammed the phone down.

She stood motionless, shaking all over, feeling Ingrid's worried eyes on her and looking to her for inspiration. 'Oh, Ingrid, what am I going to do...?'

There was nothing to be done but carry on, to go through the motions of exchanging a few words with Michael, who had, after all, travelled a long way to see her. Or so he said. She didn't doubt that he was actually in London for other reasons really, for something to do with his work.

Reluctantly he nodded in understanding when she pleaded exhaustion after a long day, explaining that she had to be up very early in the morning, which was in fact true.

'Well, when do you finish work?' he asked, glancing at the rest of them as if seeking sympathy or support or something, as if he were being hard done by. 'When can I call you?'

'I should be home around four,' she said, planning to give him a gentle brush-off. There was no way she could get involved, no way she could entertain the idea of going out with him; it would be dishonest in the extreme to give him any hope. She was in love with Stirling Robard, very deeply in love, and Michael had no chance at all with her. She recalled his crazy proposal to her in New York, and his insistence, which she had not at the time believed, that he was serious.

Dear lord, maybe he had been...

Oh, if only Stirling were that serious about her!

'Around four?' Michael glanced at his two friends. 'Well, it'll probably be a little later when I call, Becky;

we're going to be in a meeting tomorrow afternoon, I'm hoping to organise an exhibition here.'

So he was here for business reasons. Of *course* he was, Becky told herself impatiently, he had simply looked her up because he happened to be in London, that was all. With a relief that showed, she told him that was fine. 'I'll talk to you tomorrow.'

Tomorrow was Friday; she woke when it was still dark and left the flat to find a flurry of snow was falling. It was bitterly cold and she wished she could have stayed in bed all day because sleep had been impossible last night. In her opinion she was looking far from her best but the photographer with whom she worked that day raved about how good she was looking—probably to help her relax in front of the camera. It was a day that went very smoothly as far as work was concerned, all the external events of it in direct contrast to the jangled mess she was inside.

It was over, her relationship with Stirling was finished and she had to start adjusting to that fact. She just *had* to. Maybe she would go out with Michael tonight, after all? Provided she was honest with him and told him where he stood, what harm would there be in going out? Maybe they could make up a six-some with his friends and Patti and Janice? Maybe . . . no, it was not an appealing prospect, she could envisage how it would be, a riotous evening of laughing and drinking and having fun . . . which was precisely what she did not want. What she really wanted to do was to curl up and die.

She got back to the flat at just after four, as usual making herself some tea before she took off her make-up and bathed. Patti was hard on her heels, getting in at half past four and finishing off the tea that was left in the pot.

'I'll see you soon, Patti.' Becky got to her feet and stretched; there was a rule in the flat that whoever got up first got the bathroom first, whoever got home first likewise. 'Will you be wanting a bath? If so, I'll put the immersion heater on,' she offered, so there would be enough hot water to go round.

'Yes, do that, please.' There was a broad wink, a little laughter. 'I feel sure I'll be going out tonight, thought I'd get ready slowly and luxuriously.'

Becky was aching with tiredness, longing to ease her limbs in hot water, and she was doing just that when she heard the outer doorbell ring, feeling grateful that someone else was home so she didn't have to leap out and answer it.

'Becky?' There was a knock on the door, Patti's amused voice informing her that she had a visitor. 'It's Michael, just Michael—he seems to have misplaced his friends,' she added, 'which is rather a pity...'

'But—he said he'd ring.' Rebecca was irked. 'He didn't say he'd just turn up!'

'Well, he has. What shall I tell him?'

'Entertain him, Patti, give him a drink and tell him I'm in the bath. What else?'

She was out of the bath when the doorbell rang for a second time; she was in her bedroom with one leg out of her jeans and one leg in them, topless as yet and wondering who else had rolled up. Michael's friends, probably.

Her assumption was wrong. A few minutes later Patti came into the bedroom, just as Rebecca was brushing her hair. 'I'll be right with you, Patti, I'm coming now——' The look on the other girl's face made her stop. 'What is it? What's wrong?'

'I—was in the kitchen making coffee, I'm afraid Michael beat me to it and...oh, hell!'

'Oh, hell what? What on earth are you talking about, Patti?'

'It's *Stirling*! He—Michael answered the door to him and before I could get to them he was introducing himself, you know what he's like! He was slapping Stirling on the back as I came out of the kitchen, telling him that he's the friend you stayed with when you spent a week in New York.'

Becky's face went white. She lowered herself back on to the stool by the dressing-table and wondered what in heaven's name Stirling would have made of *that*!

'What are you going to do?' Patti wanted to know. 'I've been in this position myself, with two boyfriends turning up at——'

'They are *not* two boyfriends!' Becky said pointlessly, seeing the other girl's look of puzzlement. 'There was never anything between Michael and me.'

'Well, you'd better explain that to Stirling, and the sooner the better. His face is like thunder. Believe me, he does *not* look amused!'

Who was amused? Not Becky, that was for certain; she didn't know what to do, what to say, to anyone. She didn't even know why Stirling had come here.

'Becky? Honestly, I think you'd better——'

'I know.' She pushed herself to her feet, telling herself that there was only one thing she could do: she would have to play it by ear. 'Be there for me, Patti, please? Don't disappear into the bathroom just yet, will you? I need all the support I can get.'

'There's no arguing with that—of course I'll be there.'

Walking into the living-room, even with Patti on her tail, was one of the most difficult moments of Rebecca's life. Her eyes went immediately to the man who was seated by the window, motionless and silent, his face showing not the slightest flicker of emotion.

'There you are!' Michael leapt up to greet her, seeming oblivious to any awkwardness in the atmosphere. 'I was just telling your friend here about the riot we had in New York. Eh, Becky?' he added, seeking confirmation of whatever tales he had been telling.

'Yes, it was—fun,' Becky managed. She looked directly at Stirling, feeling as if she were made of jelly, and did her utmost to smile. 'Michael was kind enough to offer me a bed when—I mean, one of his beds. He—we had a lot of company, didn't we, Michael?' Frantically she turned in hope of *his* confirmation.

'Did we?'

'Yes! Of course we did! For one, there was that girl from Texas, what was her name?'

There was a split second of silence, only a split second, but it seemed to Becky to last a full hour.

'Oh, right on! Bettina. Yeah, little Bettina from Texas. She was so cute...'

Again there was silence, what seemed like another hour. The whole scene was like a tableau, nobody moved or said anything; Patti was being there but she wasn't helping at all. Not knowing what else to say, Rebecca again looked at Stirling and laughed hollowly. 'It—staying at Michael's place was like being here in many ways, there was never a moment's peace, never a time when the apartment wasn't full of friends.'

And still he said nothing. Nothing, not a single word. He just stared at her.

The ringing of the doorbell yet again broke the tension. Even Michael had become aware of it now, he was looking from Becky to Stirling with the light of comprehension in his eyes. Patti retreated to answer the door and Michael rallied. 'She's right,' he said to Stirling, 'there was never a moment's peace. I never did succeed in getting Becky to myself...' His voice trailed off, he turned to look at Becky with apology, and understanding, in his eyes. 'That's Jeff and Ken, I expect. They said they'd give me a couple of hours alone with you and then follow on——'

Becky almost screamed. Michael had just wiped out all the support he had given her, which was, apparently, more than enough for Stirling. He spoke at last. 'You wanted to have a couple of hours alone here with Rebecca, did you, Mr McCaffrey?'

'We-ll...'

'Well, you can't. Sorry about that but Rebecca is coming out with me. *Right now.*'

There was no argument—from anyone. 'Sure, anything you like,' Michael said lamely, just as the living-room was bombarded by Jeff and Ken and, coincidentally, Ingrid.

'*Rebecca.*' Stirling's voice cut across everyone else's, the warning in it unmistakable. 'Get your coat!'

Ingrid took in the entire scene with one glance and flashed a look at Becky which told her not to argue. Becky had no intention of arguing, she wanted to get out of here...but not with Stirling. That was more than she could cope with! Like a cornered animal she looked around frantically, wondering whether she could stall Stirling and make her escape on to the street.

There was no chance of that. He came over to where she was standing, standing like a piece of wood, grabbed hold of her elbow and steered her firmly into the hall. 'Your coat,' he said, snatching it from the stand. 'Put your bloody coat on and let's get *out* of here!'

CHAPTER FOURTEEN

THEY drove in silence. It was snowing heavily and the streets of London were congested with Friday night rush-hour traffic. Becky kept her eyes closed for most of the time, knowing where Stirling was taking her but not knowing what he wanted to say. She tried to convince herself that she was past caring but it didn't work. Inwardly she was a mass of nerves, her mind was re-playing the scene in the flat and she knew that Stirling had reached the obvious conclusion about her and Michael McCaffrey. She could hardly blame him; she had, after all, stayed in Michael's apartment in New York for almost a week, at his invitation, and he had been to begin with a stranger to her, a nice-looking stranger who was only five years older than she...

She closed her eyes more tightly, trying to blot out memories and wishing that her life, and her lifestyle, had been different these past few years. Then suddenly her eyes flew open and she was glaring furiously at the man by her side, her voice thick with accusation and anger. 'You think I'm going to apologise for myself, explain myself, don't you? Well, you're quite, quite wrong about that!'

Stirling said nothing. He continued to steer the Mercedes smoothly through the traffic until he was finally slipping into a space in the car park beneath the building in which his apartment was. From there he and Becky went directly into the lift in a prolonged silence which remained unbroken until they were in the privacy of his living-room. He took her coat and his own and hung them in the hall, moving from there to the kitchen. 'Would you like some coffee, Rebecca?'

'I—yes, please.' She sank into an armchair, feeling suddenly grateful to be here in spite of everything, here where it was warm and cosy and peaceful. Sanity prevailed here; at least, she hoped it would.

When Stirling emerged, she took the mug of coffee he handed her and found that she was unable to meet his eyes. He sat opposite her, on the settee, and demanded she look at him.

'Look at me,' he said, 'and answer one question for me. Just one, Rebecca.'

She looked at him, knowing what was coming. He was about to ask her to explain about Michael, about what had happened in New York, and why he was here in London now. Defiantly she raised her chin, her eyes flashing. 'No. I told you, I will not apologise for myself or for the life I've led.'

Seeing the corners of his mouth twitch was something she felt sure she had imagined. He couldn't possibly be amused, not at a moment like this. He spoke on a sigh, shocking her because he was not asking her what she had expected. 'My question is, was I right in saying what I said to you on the phone last night? Are you a virgin?'

It was happening again: she was blushing furiously and her eyes had lowered themselves; they were studying the pattern on the carpet. She didn't answer his question, but then she didn't need to.

'So that's that,' he said, sitting back in his seat and gazing at her. 'Will you marry me, Rebecca?'

Her mouth fell open, her head snapped up and she stared at him blankly, feeling breathless, trying uselessly to steady the thumping of her heart. Somehow she managed to laugh. 'Why? Because I'm a virgin?'

'No,' he said softly, with a tenderness that reached across the room to caress her. 'Because you love me.'

It was more than she could cope with. It was impossible to dissemble now, impossible to laugh, impossible to do anything but admit that he was right. 'Yes,' she whispered, glancing away again, 'I do love you.'

'And I love you. I love you more than I would have believed it possible to love someone, I love you for all that you are, for all that you have been and all that you will be. I love you today and I loved you yesterday—and tomorrow I will love you even more.'

She was crying. She had put her mug on the floor and she was crying like a child, tears streaming down her face. Her hands were poking into the pockets of her jeans but there was no handkerchief there. She took the one Stirling handed to her and wiped her face, falling into his open arms as he knelt by the chair and gathered her close. 'It's all right,' he murmured, his hand stroking her hair. 'It's all right now, my darling, now that I finally understand you.'

A minute later he was lifting her chin with his fingertips, smiling and making her look into his eyes. What she saw in them took her breath away; he did love her, he loved her every bit as much as she loved him. 'I told you yesterday that I'd reached a stage in life when there's nothing I can't handle, but I was wrong. I couldn't handle losing you, Rebecca. Please say it, say you'll marry me.'

'But, I—I don't know!' she blurted. 'You can't——'

'I'm a widower, remember?'

'I don't mean that, I mean—it's too—you've got to want it yourself, Stirling!'

'*What?*' Helplessly, he shook his head at her. 'What do you mean? What are you talking about? It's what I've always wanted!'

Incredulously, she said, 'It is? Is it? But I thought——'

'What? What did you think?'

'I thought there was no way you'd even consider marrying again, not after Angel...'

'Angel? You and she, you're chalk and cheese. I never loved Angel, I told you that.'

'I know but—but you're happy as you are, you don't need *marriage*, you can't really want that?'

'I can and I do. I need you, Rebecca. I told you there had been something missing from my life, but that I hadn't realised it. It was you, my love. Loving you has changed my life completely, I've never known anything like it. You are what's important now, and I'm sure I can make you happy. I want to marry you and make a real home with you, and children, and a truly happy life—with nothing missing. I want a love that endures, Rebecca—as ours will.' He hesitated, seeming unsure of himself, of her. 'Does—is it the idea of having children? Is that why you hesitate? Or have I misunderstood you yet again? Is it that you are the one who doesn't want marriage? It was what I assumed until very recently——'

'Me? Me! Oh, Stirling!' She nestled closely against him, her lips brushing his neck as she went on. 'It's what I want, all right, all of it, it's what I've dreamed about! Did you think I was against the idea of marriage? Is that why you asked me to live with you?'

'Of course.' He drew away, suddenly impatient with her. 'I could spank you for this, Rebecca Hill! How many times did I ask you what you wanted from life, what was important to you? I was trying to find out how you felt about marriage, what you wanted for your future. You spoke about some of your plans, about opening a boutique—but you never spoke about marriage, did you?

Did you ever speak your mind on that? Did you ever give me a straight answer?'

She bit her lip, trying hard not to laugh from sheer joy. He was right; she had never said that marriage had even entered her thinking, not for the present and not even for the future. 'I'll give you a straight answer now,' she told him, moving closer in order to kiss him. 'I will marry you, my darling, just as soon as it can be arranged.'

HARLEQUIN
Romance®

announces

The Bridal Collection

one special Romance
every month,
featuring
a Bride, a Groom and a Wedding!

Beginning in May 1992
with
The Man You'll Marry
by Debbie Macomber

WED-1

HARLEQUIN PROUDLY PRESENTS A
DAZZLING CONCEPT IN ROMANCE FICTION

One small town,
twelve terrific love stories.

TYLER—GREAT READING...GREAT SAVINGS...
AND A FABULOUS FREE GIFT

Each book set in Tyler is a self-contained love story;
together, the twelve novels stitch the fabric of
the community.

By collecting proofs-of-purchase found in each Tyler
book, you can receive a fabulous gift, ABSOLUTELY
FREE! And use our special Tyler coupons to save on
your next Tyler book purchase.

Join us for the third Tyler book, WISCONSIN
WEDDING by Carla Neggers, available in May.

Janet Dailey's perennially popular Americana series continues with more exciting states!

Don't miss this romantic tour of America through fifty favorite Harlequin Presents novels, each one set in a different state, and researched by Janet and her husband, Bill.

A journey of a lifetime in one cherished collection.

Following the success of WITH THIS RING,
Harlequin cordially invites you to enjoy the
romance of the wedding season with

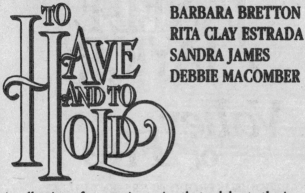

BARBARA BRETTON
RITA CLAY ESTRADA
SANDRA JAMES
DEBBIE MACOMBER

A collection of romantic stories that celebrate the joy,
excitement, and mishaps of planning that special day
by these four award-winning Harlequin authors.

**Available in April at your favorite Harlequin
retail outlets.**

THTH

❧ Harlequin®

JANELLE TAYLOR

Valley of *Fire*

HARLEQUIN IS PROUD TO PRESENT *VALLEY OF FIRE* BY JANELLE TAYLOR—AUTHOR OF TWENTY-TWO BOOKS, INCLUDING SIX *NEW YORK TIMES* BESTSELLERS

VALLEY OF FIRE—the warm and passionate story of Kathy Alexander, a famous romance author, and Steven Winngate, entrepreneur and owner of the magazine that intended to expose the real Kathy "Brandy" Alexander to her fans.

Don't miss VALLEY OF FIRE, available in May.